Just when Raine thought maybe he was rethinking the whole cop thing and having her arrested, his gaze met hers again.

The look of concern had been replaced with one of determination.

"You wanted to meet with me," Callum said. "Here's your chance. And the only reason I'm giving it to you is because your gun wasn't loaded. Start talking."

She bristled at his command. "I don't see the point in pleading my case. The police are going to throw me in jail when they get here."

"Not if I don't press charges."

She hesitated. Was this a trick? "Why would you change your mind now?"

The man named Asher nodded in agreement. "Good question. She abducted you, Callum. Held you at gunpoint and handcuffed you to a chair. Whether the gun was loaded or not is irrelevant."

"What she did was reprehensible," Callum admitted, "but I wasn't hurt. And we both have something each other needs. I want the name of that killer. She wants my help to save her brother."

THE SECRET SHE KEEPS

LENA DIAZ

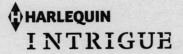

To Lisa and Laura, the sisters I would have chosen even if we
weren't related. Together we will survive, overcome and learn
how to navigate our new normal. Love will get us through.
Laughter is just around the corner. Fake it until you make it.
Love you. Always. Forever.

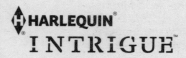

Recycling programs
for this product may
not exist in your area.

ISBN-13: 978-1-335-59123-4

The Secret She Keeps

For questions and comments about the quality of this book,
please contact us at CustomerService@Harlequin.com.

Harlequin Enterprises ULC
22 Adelaide St. West, 41st Floor
Toronto, Ontario M5H 4E3, Canada
www.Harlequin.com

Printed in U.S.A.

Lena Diaz was born in Kentucky and has also lived in California, Louisiana and Florida, where she now resides with her husband and two children. Before becoming a romantic suspense author, she was a computer programmer. A Romance Writers of America Golden Heart® Award finalist, she has also won the prestigious Daphne du Maurier Award for Excellence in Mystery/Suspense. To get the latest news about Lena, please visit her website, lenadiaz.com.

Visit the Author Profile page at Harlequin.com.

CAST OF CHARACTERS

Callum Wright—Investigator for the civilian cold-case company Unfinished Business. He's helping Raine investigate her brother's cold case in exchange for information on the serial killer he's trying to catch.

Raine Quintero—With her brother's scheduled execution looming, this business lawyer will do anything to save him, including making a deal with the man who helped send him to death row: Callum Wright.

Joey Quintero—Raine's brother was convicted of murder and sentenced to death. Is he innocent? And is his case connected to Callum's hunt for a serial killer?

Faith Lancaster—Fellow UB cold-case investigator, she's also something Raine never expected—an ally.

Asher Whitfield—Faith's partner in the search for a serial killer, his distrust of Raine could destroy her chance to save her brother.

Pete Scoggin—Recent attacks on Raine could be the serial killer. Is it Pete? Or someone else entirely?

Chapter One

In a Smoky Mountains parking lot high above Gatlinburg, Tennessee, Raine Quintero watched for her prey through the windshield. Clutched in her hands was the unregistered nine-millimeter pistol she'd bought in the back room of a sleazy bar a week earlier.

As plans went, hers wasn't exactly inspired. The chance of success was probably fifty-fifty, at best. But everything else she'd tried had failed. She was out of options, desperate and almost out of time. Desperation, like grief, had stages. Reaching this final stage had taken fifteen agonizing years. Now she was prepared to do anything, cross any line, pay any price to save her brother's life.

Even if it meant threatening someone else's.

An inconvenient twinge of decency and shame had the pistol shaking in her hands. Like a thousand jagged knives, her conscience slashed through her carefully constructed excuses for what she was about to do. She rocked back and forth in her seat, a roller coaster of emotions twisting inside her. When a hot tear rolled down her cheek and dripped onto her hand, she swore and shoved the pistol inside the glove box.

Apparently, Callum Wright would get one last chance. He could act, or refuse to act. His fate would be decided by his choice.

Unlike her brother, who'd never been given a choice.

Clenching her now empty hands together, she drew deep, even breaths until the shaking subsided. The guilt was still there. But she'd managed to force it back into its little box to be dealt with later. This didn't change her overall plan. She hadn't come here on a whim. Everything had led to this one crucial moment. Sometimes the end really did justify the means.

Or so she kept telling herself.

Blowing out another deep breath, she checked the time on the fitness tracker on her wrist. If this morning was like the last few, the man who held her brother's fate in his hands would be here in just a few more minutes.

Sure enough, at precisely seven thirty, Callum's black Lexus all-wheel-drive SUV turned into the parking lot of the company where he worked, Unfinished Business. It always took her aback when she saw him driving that type of vehicle. Although nice, it didn't cost anywhere near what he could afford.

From what she'd gleaned about UB, the company paid its investigators extremely well. It's how the billionaire owner had attracted top detectives around the country to give up their government jobs and switch to the private sector. It helped explain why Callum had traded life near his family in Athens, Georgia, to live in the Smoky Mountains of Gatlinburg, Tennessee. Although, surprisingly, none of her internet searches had ever revealed his exact address, either when he'd lived in Georgia or after he'd moved here.

His Lexus certainly didn't compare to her red Porsche Panamera sports car back home. Of course, that wasn't what she was driving today. Her mission required something easily forgettable that blended in. She'd bought a rusty, midnight blue, decade-old Ford Taurus the same day she'd bought the gun. Cash, of course. Nine thousand dollars—purposely below the government's ten-thousand-dollar threshold that would have triggered a report to the IRS or even a money-laundering investigation. She didn't want to raise any red flags.

The parking lot was almost full, so Callum backed into a space at the far right corner shaded by thick trees and overgrown shrubs. Some of those trees concealed a steep drop-off down the side of Prescott Mountain, named after the owner of Unfinished Business. She knew about that drop-off because she'd hiked through those woods several times, learning the geography, planning her emergency escape route if it came to that. She didn't anticipate needing it. Her hope was that Callum would be decent and reasonable.

Unlike Isaac Farley, a police detective with whom he'd once worked.

Raine's Taurus was parked on the opposite end of the parking lot, close to the building but concealed from prying eyes by the dazzling golden leaves of a hickory tree fully dressed for autumn. It also gave her a good vantage point to watch Callum long before he'd notice her.

She'd spent many hours over the past week in this parking lot, or in the surrounding forest doing reconnaissance. So far, she'd never seen anyone pull in later than eight. That wasn't typical of the firm where she worked. Although she and the other lawyers always arrived before sunrise and left around dinnertime, the administrative staff tended to mosey in closer to nine and weren't fans of working late. It would be nice to know how the bosses here motivated their staff so she could motivate her own the same way.

Not that she planned on going back.

What she was doing today would change everything. Best case, it would get her disbarred and end her career. Worst case, she'd go to prison. But she wasn't even tempted not to follow through. This was far more important than a future partnership in a law firm. Her goal was worth any sacrifice. There would be no regrets.

Callum finally got out of his vehicle. He must have been delayed by a call since he was on the phone when he shut the car door. His long strides quickly carried him toward the building as he slid his cell phone into his suit jacket pocket.

She couldn't help admiring his taste in clothes.

The navy blue suit and matching tie with a crisp white shirt accentuated his impressively broad shoulders and trim waist. But, as with his car, his suit was a nice quality but didn't seem overly expensive. There wasn't the flash of a gold Rolex on his wrist or pricey rings either. The most expensive things he was wearing were probably his pristine black cowboy boots.

To the untrained eye, they weren't anything special. But she could spot high-quality handmade leather a mile away. Her mom had always told her she could judge a man by the quality and cleanliness of his shoes. Raine preferred to judge a man by how he treated others.

And today was judgment day.

He was almost to her car when she got out, tugging her gray sweater into place against the chilly mountain air. As she rounded the hood, he smiled and nodded in greeting but continued past her.

"Mr. Wright?"

He stopped and walked back, a dark brow arched in question. "Good morning. My apologies, but I don't recall your name." He held out his hand.

She shook it, encouraged that he was talking to her. "We haven't met before. I'm Raine Quintero." She waited for a sign of recognition. Sadly, her last name didn't even trigger a flicker of reaction.

"How can I help you, Ms. Quintero?"

"I've been trying to reach you about investigating a case for me. But your office manager is a bit of a bulldog about putting me through on the phone. I'm guessing since you haven't returned any of my calls that she hasn't given you my messages."

He grimaced. "Sorry about that. We recently hired more administrative staff out of necessity. Our company's success has resulted in a flood of calls and visits off the street that were interfering with our ability to focus on our investigations. I'm guessing she told you we partner with law enforcement to try to solve the cold cases that they don't have the resources to work."

"She did. And I understand your company's charter. I've read the disclaimers on their website. But this is different, critically important. My brother was sent to prison thirteen years ago for a crime he didn't commit. It's urgent that I—"

He held up his hand to stop her. "Ms. Quintero, my sympathies about your brother, truly. But we can't help you. Our contracts are with the various law enforcement agencies of east Tennessee, including TBI—the Tennessee Bureau of Investigation. We don't hire out to private individuals."

"Your company just finished a case for a civilian, a nurse, Skylar Montgomery. I saw a story about it on the news. If you made an exception for her, you can make one for me. I want to hire *you*. Money isn't an issue. I can afford whatever fees you charge."

He shook his head. "It's not about money. Ms. Montgomery's situation was unique, a one-off. I'm not sure why you're singling me out, specifically. But it doesn't change anything."

"I would hope my brother being on death row would change *everything*. I really need your help."

His jaw tightened. "If he's on death row, you need an attorney who specializes in capital punishment cases. Again, I'm sorry." He started past her again.

"Joey Quintero. Ring a bell?"

He stopped and turned around, his expression beginning to mirror impatience. "No, but I'm guessing you think it should."

She hurried to him, craning her neck back to meet his dark blue gaze. "You worked on his case when you were a police detective in Athens, Georgia. *That's* why I singled you out."

His expression turned thoughtful. "Thirteen years ago?"

"Fifteen when the case began. He was accused of strangling a young woman in her home, when her parents were out of town. Capital murder, death row, Quintero. You honestly don't remember?"

He stared off into space as if accessing off-site storage in his mental memory banks. The flash of recognition she'd been hoping to see finally happened. But the frown that accompanied it told her she wasn't going to like what he was about to say.

"My recollection is spotty on that case. As you said, it was a long time ago. And I wouldn't have been a lead detective back then."

"Farley was."

He slowly nodded. "Farley. Haven't heard that name in a while."

His flat tone suggested that he and Farley hadn't exactly been friends. That was encouraging.

"He passed away a few years ago," she told him. "Massive heart attack. But I did get to speak to him before that. Or, I tried. Several times. He told me to go to hell."

"Sounds like Farley."

"And now you're telling me to do the same."

"No. I've been politely explaining why I can't hire out to investigate for you. For one thing, the company I work for only handles cases for the eastern Tennessee region, not Georgia. That's part of our contract with the various counties we support. But even if I wanted to work independently, outside of my company, I don't have any unique insight into what happened that could help with an appeal. I was a brand-new detective, more of a gopher than a true investigator. Farley didn't involve me in the guts of any of the cases he was working. He had me do research on case law, minor witness interviews, follow up on calls to our crime tip line. Your brother confessed, didn't he? Seems like I remember that much."

"It was coerced, a false confession."

"That's hard to believe, considering that our interrogations were supposed to be recorded to protect against that sort of thing. Did his attorney review the recording and argue that his confession should be thrown out?"

"His defense attorney was an idiot."

"I'll take that as a no. Look, I'm sorry that you and your family are suffering—"

"What family, Mr. Wright? My parents died in a car wreck four years ago. My brother's all I have and he's going to be executed in a matter of weeks unless I can find someone who can provide some kind of evidence, some kind of doubt, that could be used for a grant of clemency. I'm truly out of options or I wouldn't be here talking to one of the people responsible for sending an innocent man to prison in the first place."

He sighed deeply. "Ms. Quintero, if you knew me at all, you'd know that I'm a man who values honesty, integrity and justice over winning percentages. I live by the judicial system's golden rule, that everyone's innocent *unless* proven guilty. From what I'm starting to remember of the Quintero case, it was solid. Didn't the jury deliberate for just a few hours before returning with a guilty verdict?"

"Only because his attorney was incompetent. He put up a pathetic defense. My brother didn't hurt anyone."

His gaze hardened. "Tell that to the victim's family."

She grabbed his arm when he would have turned to leave. "Please, all I'm asking is for a meeting with you. An hour of your time to review—"

He gently but firmly pushed her hand away. "I don't get guilty people out of prison. That's what lawyers are for."

She sucked in a sharp breath at his insult to her profession. But before she could gather her composure to try again, he was rapidly striding away. His shiny boots flashed in the morning sun as he jogged up the front steps of UB headquarters and disappeared inside the glass-and-steel building.

Raine swore beneath her breath and hopped in her car. She glanced longingly at the glove box, then started the engine. Callum Wright had made his choice. He'd judged her brother guilty. But it was Callum who was guilty—of not caring that he'd helped send an innocent man to death row. If she didn't do everything she could to correct that travesty, she'd be just as responsible for her brother's plight as Callum and Farley.

Her inconvenient conscience wasn't bothering her now. If anything, she was more determined than ever to follow through with her plan. Callum hadn't stopped her. He'd only delayed her.

Raine forced herself to slowly drive out of the parking lot even though she wanted to stomp the accelerator. As soon as she was out of sight of the building and reached the first cut-out area designed for sightseers or someone with car trouble, she pulled over.

All around her the infamous mist that gave the Smokies their name rose in white puffs like ancient smoke signals. But it did little to obscure the brilliant reds and golds that dressed the mountains in their spectacular autumn glory. At any other time, she'd have been awestruck by such beauty. But she wasn't here to enjoy the view. Grabbing her black backpack from the rear seat, she stowed her gun inside then got out.

A few moments later she'd made her way through the woods to the edge of the parking lot of Unfinished Business. When she reached the trees directly behind Callum's SUV, she located a bush that provided good cover along with a decent view through some gaps in the branches. In addition to his Lexus, she could see straight down the aisle to the front doors of UB headquarters. She pulled out her gun and used her backpack as a rather uncomfortable chair. But it beat sitting directly on the cold ground.

After assuming she'd be waiting most of the day for Callum to leave the building again, she was pleasantly surprised to see him heading toward her just a few hours later. A navy blue backpack was slung over one shoulder, the modern equivalent of the briefcases that executives carried decades earlier.

Was he on his way to meet someone? Or planning to take home some files to review in private instead of in the office? She hoped it was the latter. That would give her more time to do what she had to do before anyone realized he was missing.

Hefting the pistol in her left hand, she crept as close to the SUV's bumper as she dared. As soon as he slid into the driver's seat, she rushed to the open doorway, aiming her gun at him while she desperately tried not to shake too noticeably.

His blue eyes darkened with anger as he looked at the gun, then at her. "Ms. Quintero. Mind telling me what the hell you're doing?"

"We're about to have that meeting I requested. Very slowly, no sudden moves, take your gun out using only two fingers and pitch it onto the passenger floorboard."

"What makes you think I have a gun?"

"Don't play games. I've been watching you for a while. I've figured out you have a holster under that suit jacket. Toss it."

His eyes narrowed dangerously, but he did as she asked. "Now what?"

His hard expression and clipped tone had her hands shaking even harder. She pushed one of the buttons on his door, unlocking the rest of the doors.

"If you honk the horn, flash your lights or do anything else to attract attention, you'll earn a bullet. And anyone you alert will get shot too. Understood?"

His jaw tightened. "Understood."

She yanked open the door behind him and hopped inside. "Close your door."

As he pulled it closed, she quickly fastened her seat belt then brought up her gun again. A bead of sweat ran down the side of her face in spite of the chilly interior of his SUV. She pressed the bore of the pistol hard against his seat. "Feel that?"

"I assume that's your gun pushing against my back."

"You assume correctly. Start the engine."

The SUV roared to life. As he reached for his seat belt, she shoved the pistol harder against his chair.

"No seat belt."

His angry gaze met hers in the rearview mirror. "Why?"

"If you don't have your seat belt on, you'll think

twice about pulling some stunt, like purposely wrecking to try to get away. Pull out of the parking lot, slowly. Don't draw any attention."

He hesitated.

She swallowed hard, wincing as she moved the gun to the back of his head.

He swore and slowly pulled out of the parking space.

Chapter Two

Callum took a quick glance at his rearview mirror as he maneuvered his SUV down the narrow two-lane road that wound around Prescott Mountain. Had there been another car back there at the last curve? Had someone been in the parking lot and saw what was happening? Or was it just the sun casting shadows through the trees?

"Slow down," Quintero warned.

Her pistol was still pushing against his seat. Barely enough to feel the pressure against his back, but enough to remind him it was there.

"If we end up in a ditch, I swear I'll shoot you." Her voice was as shaky as her hands had been on her gun earlier.

She probably *would* shoot him if he wrecked, whether she meant to or not. She didn't have the sense to keep her finger on the gun's frame instead of the trigger to avoid accidentally firing the pistol. That was the first thing he'd noticed when she'd stood in his open door. It was the only reason he hadn't immediately tackled her.

"I mean it." She jabbed the pistol harder. "Be careful."

"I'll slow down when you quit digging your gun into my back. And while we're at it, unless you plan on shooting me while I'm driving, move your finger from the trigger to the gun frame. It's safer that way. For both of us."

In the rearview mirror he caught her look of surprise. She glanced down, presumably at her gun. The pressure on his back eased. He hoped that meant she'd moved her finger off the trigger too. She was obviously a novice around guns, which only made her more dangerous.

As they passed the turnoff he'd have taken to go home, he eased his foot off the accelerator, slowing down as she'd requested. It wasn't necessary. He knew every curve of this mountain and how fast he could safely go without skidding into a guardrail. Wherever she lived there must not be any mountains, as skittish as she seemed.

"Better?" He gentled his voice, wanting her to feel less threatened, less anxious, even though he intended to take that gun away from her at the first viable opportunity.

She wiped some sweat from her brow. "Better." Her striking green eyes met his in the rearview mirror. "Thank you," she added grudgingly, as if she couldn't help herself.

He nodded, noting that her hand had still been shaking when she'd wiped her brow. Abducting people wasn't something she was comfortable with. He wished he'd researched her after their brief discussion earlier this morning. If he had, he'd at least have some background information. Maybe he could have used that to his advantage. But he'd forgotten about her when he'd stepped inside and fellow investigator Asher Whitfield had pulled him into a meeting about the serial killer cold case they were working together.

Given her brother's history, it was surprising that there was nothing about Raine that screamed criminal. In his experience, when one sibling was a murderer, the other was often intimately familiar with the wrong side of the law as well. And yet, he was willing to bet the most serious offense on her record before today was speeding.

In spite of his anger over her putting him in this situation, he couldn't help admiring her loyalty to her family and her willingness to risk everything to try to save her brother. Too bad for her that saving him was probably impossible.

Thirteen years on death row meant he'd likely exhausted most, if not all, of his appeals. His last resort would be a grant of clemency from the governor—assuming the governor of Georgia had that authority. Callum wasn't familiar with Georgia's laws regarding overturning convictions or granting stays of execution. As a cop, his focus had always been on putting the bad guys away, not getting them out.

That's what lawyers did.

He didn't know why she believed he might be able to even speak to anyone with authority over her brother's situation. Politicians weren't part of his social circle. And he didn't know the governor of *any* state.

His friend Noah Reid might have some pull with the governor of Georgia. He held an executive position in their Department of Corrections. But was Reid in a position to influence the fate of a death row inmate? Callum rather doubted it.

His boss, Grayson Prescott, had a handful of governors on speed dial and no doubt held considerable sway. But any hope that he'd speak on Raine's brother's behalf had ended the second she'd pulled a gun on one of his investigators.

Regret gnawed at Callum as he glanced at her in the mirror. Her shoulder-length dark hair accentuated her pale complexion. She was obviously scared, even though she was the one with the gun. She must have felt like she had no choice after he'd refused to give her one hour of his time. That's all she'd requested. And he'd been too busy to bother. Maybe this was his wake-up call to pay more attention to the pain of those around him instead of immersing himself in his work. Too bad it had come too late to save Raine Quintero from the consequences of her rather drastic actions.

They were getting close to the bottom of the mountain. Soon, the road would end and he'd have to turn. Left, toward town, where the tourists were no doubt clogging River Road, frequenting the little shops and restaurants. Or they could turn right toward the more rural part of the area without the kinds of attractions that drew hordes of out-of-towners.

To Callum's thinking, the rural part was the most beautiful and worth seeing. But if that's where she wanted to go, it meant driving farther away from the possibility of someone noticing them and realizing he was in trouble.

Unless the shadow on the road earlier wasn't a shadow.

He checked the rearview mirror again. No one behind them. Raine's reflection showed her frowning, then glancing over her shoulder.

"What are you looking at?" she asked.

"You. We're going to come to a stop sign soon. It would be easier for me to drive if I know where to go."

Her frown eased. "West. Turn right at the sign."

He nodded, unsurprised but disappointed. Without the sights and sounds of traffic and people around, it would be harder to catch her off guard. Then again, it also meant less risk to innocent bystanders, so it was probably for the best. He'd bide his time, do what he could to keep her calm and thinking she was completely in control of the situation.

Then he'd take her gun.

His cell phone beeped in his pocket.

She sat up straighter. "What's that?"

He sighed and pulled out the phone. "Someone's calling from the office. If I don't answer, they'll get suspicious."

She chewed her bottom lip, then pressed the gun into the back of the seat again. "Remember what I said. Your life, and the life of anyone you try to warn, is at risk. Put the call on speaker and get off as quickly as possible, without pulling any stunts."

Being on speaker would make it difficult to alert anyone. He'd have to wing it and see if there was anything he could do to let them know he was in trouble and where he was. He pressed the speaker button on the phone and held it up in the air beside him.

"Callum. You're on speaker."

"Hey, it's Thomas. Everything okay? I thought we were going to review those files at your house, but you're either not home or ignoring the doorbell."

He glanced at Raine before answering. "Sorry, forgot I had another appointment out of town."

The gun shoved harder against the seat at his *out of town* reference. She was smart. He'd have to remember that.

"I won't be back for a while," he said. "You might as well head to your house and start without me." Which would take him in the same direction that she'd just told Callum to go.

"Do you have an ETA on when I can expect you?" Thomas asked.

Raine shook her head, her hair bouncing on her shoulders.

"Hard to say. I really couldn't guess," Callum answered.

She made a rolling motion with her right hand, letting him know to hurry. They'd just reached the stop sign so he braked and made sure no one was coming before pulling out.

"I've got to go, Thomas. Again, sorry for the mix-up. Talk to you later." He pressed a button on the side of the phone and set it in the console, facedown.

She let out a deep breath, an expression of relief on her face.

"Where to now, Ms. Quintero? Or should I call you Raine? If you're trusting me to help your brother, we should be on a first-name basis."

"We're not friends. Ms. Quintero is fine." She motioned toward the road. "Just keep going straight. I'll let you know when to turn again."

"Can you at least give me a guesstimate on mileage? I've got less than a quarter tank of gas."

She leaned over, peering at the dash. "What kind of miles-per-gallon does this thing get?"

"I've probably got enough fuel to go about seventy miles, give or take. Half that if this is a round trip. Less if we climb up into the mountains."

"We should be okay. We've only got about twelve more miles to go and we're staying in the valley."

When she sat back, he glanced toward his phone to double-check that the screen wasn't visible. He didn't want her to realize that all he'd done was press the button to silence the ringer. He hadn't ended the call.

And he didn't work with anyone named Thomas.

Chapter Three

The closer they got to the turnoff, the more Raine began to think she'd made a terrible mistake. Not in getting him to meet with her. She needed to show him the evidence she had, tell him her hopes for freeing Joey. But even though *how* she was carrying out this plan had made sense on paper, the reality felt entirely different.

For one thing, Callum was much more intimidating up close than she'd expected. He made her nervous. Not just because he was so much taller than her, and so obviously stronger. The real problem was that she liked him. He'd made her angry when he'd refused to meet with her. But aside from that, he'd been polite, even kind. He wasn't trying to scare her. And aside from initially pretending he didn't have a gun—which was understandable—he hadn't pulled any tricks even though she knew she would have in his situation.

If she hadn't known he'd been involved in sending her brother to death row, she'd have thought he was a decent guy. Heck, she'd have been all over him. He was the epitome of tall, dark and handsome. Exactly her type.

That was a problem.

She needed to focus. But seeing him as a *man*, and as a surprisingly decent person, was making it difficult to continue to treat him so deplorably. Her actions seemed…evil, even though her goal—saving a life—was anything but evil. Still, she'd gone too far down this path to stop now. Being awful to Callum was something she'd have to learn to forgive herself for, eventually. But if Joey died, and she hadn't done everything she could to prevent his death, she'd *never* forgive herself for that.

A flash of color through the windshield had her shaking herself from her thoughts. "See that yellow sign up there? The one with the squiggles on it?"

He smiled in the rearview mirror. "The one warning that the road ahead has lots of tight curves?"

Her face heated. "The turn is just before it, on the left. It's a private driveway. The brush is overgrown, which makes it hard to find. You'll have to slow down."

"I see it."

He turned into the narrow dirt-and-gravel driveway. Raine winced as the tree branches on either side made sickening metallic scraping sounds whenever they came into contact with the sides of his vehicle. Regardless of today's outcome, she owed him a paint job.

About fifty yards later the driveway ended in front of a small, one-story clapboard house. The flaking yellowed paint had probably been white at one time. Gingerbread millwork beneath the sagging porch roof proclaimed that someone had loved this home once, long before it had been abandoned and left to rot.

"Cut the engine," she told him.

"We're actually going inside that thing?"

"It's not as bad as you think. I cleaned out the animal droppings and squirrel nests. At least I think they were squirrels."

"Wonderful."

She hopped out and yanked open his door just in time to see him grabbing his cell phone.

"Toss the phone on the floorboard," she ordered, quickly backing out of his reach.

He sighed and pitched it beside his discarded pistol. "You know, it's really not necessary to keep pointing your gun at me."

"I wish I could believe that." She moved farther away, both hands on the pistol grip. "Into the house, please."

He stepped down from the SUV. "I'll listen to whatever you have to say. Put the gun down first."

"Inside. Then we'll talk."

She needed him in the house to give her an advantage. Out here, the trees offered too many hiding places if he made a run for it. Inside the dilapidated structure she had better control over what happened. She just needed to keep her pistol pointed at him and stay out of his reach. He looked like he wanted to pounce on her. Not in a good way.

He paused at the bottom of the steps, testing one with his foot as if worried that it might not support his weight.

"It's safe," she assured him. "I checked the beams underneath. The boards are weathered but solid."

He nodded his thanks and headed up the stairs. She winced as he pushed the front door open and it creaked like something in an old horror movie. Behind him, she set her backpack on the wooden floor and closed the door. He stopped halfway into the room and looked around.

There wasn't much to see.

It was small and nearly empty. The grimy windows had no coverings, so the sunlight filtering through the trees overhead illuminated the place well enough. If he'd smelled it before she'd cleaned it, he'd have fallen over. She was pretty sure feral cats had taken up residence. Even now, essence of wild animals was still detectable. But it was bearable.

The kitchen, with its sagging cabinets and lack of appliances, was visible through a doorway on the left. There were two small bedrooms down the middle hallway, not that he would know that since the doors were closed. What mattered was what was sitting in the middle of the main room—a wooden chair she'd dragged in from the back porch. A pair of handcuffs dangled from each of the arms.

"Take a seat," she said behind him, careful to keep her distance.

He slowly walked to the chair. But when he reached it, he turned to face her. "You're not handcuffing me."

"You're right. I'm not. You are." She raised the pistol, proud of herself for not shaking this time. And she kept her finger on the frame as he'd cautioned earlier, to make him less worried. "I don't want to hurt you. I truly don't. But I won't mourn your loss if you force me to shoot. After all, if it wasn't for you and Farley, my brother wouldn't be on death row."

He stared at her a long moment as if weighing her resolve. Then he sat.

She let out a relieved breath. Almost there. "Left- or right-handed?" she asked.

"Left."

Figuring he was lying, she said, "Fasten the cuff on your right wrist."

He chuckled. "Don't believe me, huh?"

"Nope."

He pulled the cuff that was open and dangling from the chair arm and fastened it on his wrist.

She slowly moved forward, the pistol never wavering. But instead of getting in front of him, she moved behind him and peered over his right shoulder. He raised his arm and shook the chain, proving it was fastened securely.

"Pull the other one up and work your left wrist inside the cuff."

"Kind of hard to do with only one free hand."

"Put the cuff on your thigh for leverage. The chain's long enough. Once it's around your wrist, press against your thigh to ratchet it."

He tried to look at her over his shoulder but she'd stepped back again. "You put a lot of thought into this."

"I always do when something's important." She'd actually cuffed herself to the chair, only one arm at a time, of course, trying it out. She'd been able to do it and had no doubt he could too.

He sighed and did as she asked.

Again, she leaned slightly over his shoulder to make sure he'd truly fastened the cuff. When she saw that he had, the tension in her shoulders eased. Now she was safe and she had a captive audience— literally. He had no choice but to listen to her.

"Now we can talk. I'll grab my folder."

She shoved her pistol in the waistband of her jeans, then retrieved a two-inch-thick folder from her backpack. It was the only one she'd brought with her on this little escapade. Just enough information to whet his appetite. If he agreed to her terms, she'd give him four more folders thicker than this one, with a lot more detail.

As she hurried toward him, she couldn't help smiling. For the first time in a long time, she had hope for the future. For Joey's future.

"I've been working on this for over a year," she said. "Nights, weekends, vacations. Even hired a few private investigators for some of it." She grimaced. "Can't say I'd recommend them. They'd fail miserably at your company. Not at all the caliber that UB hires, from what I've heard." She pulled out one of the summary sheets. "Regardless of how you feel about my brother, I guarantee you'll want to see this." She set it on his lap.

He suddenly grabbed the arms of the chair and

swept out his right leg. She squeaked in surprise as his foot hooked behind her knees, dumping her backward onto the hard wood floor. Her head made a sickening crack and everything went blurry. She winced at the awful, throbbing pain in her skull and desperately tried to focus. When she did, Callum was standing a few feet away holding the chair up in the air.

She screamed and covered her head, certain her life was about to end with a brutally violent blow. Instead, the chair crashed against the floor a few feet away in an explosion of sound. Pieces of wood pinged off the walls and floor. Sawdust and papers rained down like dirty snowflakes.

She was alive. He hadn't hurt her, even though her throbbing head disagreed. Just as it occurred to her to reach for her gun, he was on top of her, pinning her wrists above her head. She stared up at him, her muddled mind still struggling to understand what had happened.

"Next time you abduct someone," he told her, his tone matter-of-fact as if he wasn't practically crushing her, "secure their legs too."

The door flew open and slammed against the wall. Raine jerked against him, her body trembling as half a dozen people ran inside. As one, they surrounded the two of them and aimed their pistols at her head.

Callum grinned at the man standing to his right. "Took you long enough."

"Yeah, well. Your directions were lousy."

Callum laughed as he looked down again. "Raine

Quintero, meet *Thomas*. Except his real name is Asher Whitfield. All of these men and women are investigators at Unfinished Business. We have each other's backs. Always. Consider yourself under citizen's arrest until we get the cops here."

To her horror, tears started coursing down her cheeks. She drew a shaky breath and tried to reason with him. "Please, Callum. If you send me to jail, you might as well execute my brother yourself."

His smile faded and he stood, pulling her to standing. She winced and grabbed her head. It felt as if someone was hammering it from inside her skull. There was a tug at her waistband and she realized that he'd taken her pistol. He handed it to one of his teammates.

"Handcuff key." He held out his hand toward her, the remaining pieces of a chair arm dangling from the chain around his wrist.

Trying desperately to ignore the crushing pain in her head, she pulled the key out of her front jeans pocket and gave it to him. As he stepped back to unlock the cuffs, two of his teammates grabbed her arms. Not that it mattered. She could barely stand, let alone run away. The room kept tilting at crazy angles. No doubt she had a concussion, maybe worse. If she threw up, she hoped she was fortunate enough to do it on Callum's shoes.

"This isn't even loaded." The teammate who'd taken her gun from Callum held up the magazine. "Empty. And there's nothing in the chamber."

Callum stared at her incredulously. "You abducted

me with an unloaded gun? What were you thinking? I could have killed you."

"It was my choice to risk my own life. But it wouldn't have been right to risk anyone else's."

"You bluffed. Knowing I likely had a loaded gun." He couldn't seem to get past that fact.

She nodded, then winced at the pounding in her head.

He swore.

"Hey, Callum." Asher stood with some of her papers that he'd scooped off the floor. "These aren't documents about her brother that I heard you mention on the phone." His expression mirrored his surprise. "They're about the serial killer you and I have been investigating for the past few months. And this…" He held up one of the pages. "This is about a murder we've never even connected to the others, one that she attributes to the same killer. It says she's figured out a viable suspect for the murders. His name's right here. Except that it's written in some kind of code."

The room fell silent and everyone stared at her.

Callum's expression was a mixture of shock and admiration. "Is that true? You know the killer's identity? The one who's murdered five people in east Tennessee over the past decade?"

"Eight. Not five." In spite of the sickening way the room kept pitching back and forth, she forced her chin up a notch. "That was my bargaining chip. I was going to share my research with you to try to make a deal so you'd help me save my brother. But it's too late now. The cops are on their way."

He stared at her a long moment, then glanced questioningly at a young blonde woman. "Faith?"

"I called 911 as soon as we had the room secured." She chuckled. "Or, rather, as soon as *you* had it secured. You didn't end up needing the cavalry after all."

He smiled, but his smile faded when he looked down at Raine again. Instead, his brow furrowed with worry. "Faith. Call an ambulance. She doesn't look so good."

He motioned to the people holding her arms and they slowly lowered her to sit on the floor. The room wasn't spinning quite as badly now. She aimed a look of gratitude at him, not willing to risk something as painful as nodding. "I don't suppose you could have Faith cancel the police request when she asks for that ambulance."

He crouched and reached for her. She ducked to avoid his hand, sucking in a sharp breath when it made her head throb anew.

Swearing, he said, "Be still. I'm not going to hurt you."

She froze and allowed him to feel along the back of her head. His touch was incredibly careful, gentle. But the moment his fingers brushed where she'd cracked her skull against the floor, pain lanced through her. She winced and ducked away.

"I'm sorry, Raine. I didn't mean to cause you more pain."

His contrite tone and the concerned look on his face told her he genuinely meant what he'd said.

Which made her even more confused. She'd been awful to him. And here he was concerned about her. That guilt that she'd thought she'd locked away was roaring back now, making her face heat with embarrassment. "I know. Thanks. I'm okay."

"You're definitely not okay. You've got quite a lump there. Probably a concussion. No blood though. Your scalp isn't lacerated. No need for stitches."

"Thank God for small favors I suppose."

He glanced at the blonde woman again, Faith. She gave him a small nod, as if to assure him the ambulance was on the way.

Just when Raine thought maybe he was rethinking the whole cop thing and having her arrested, his gaze met hers again. The look of concern had been replaced with one of determination.

"You wanted to meet with me," he said. "Here's your chance. The only reason I'm giving it to you is because your gun wasn't loaded. Start talking."

She bristled at his command. "I don't see the point in pleading my case. The police are going to throw me in jail when they get here."

"Not if I don't press charges."

She hesitated. Was this a trick? "Why would you change your mind now?"

The man named Asher nodded in agreement. "Good question. She abducted you, Callum. Held you at gunpoint and handcuffed you to a chair. Whether the gun was loaded or not is irrelevant."

"What she did was reprehensible," Callum agreed. "But I wasn't hurt. And we both have something each other needs. I want the name of that killer. She wants my help to save her brother. Faith, how long before the police arrive?"

"I'd guess ten minutes, give or take."

"The clock's ticking, Raine. I need a name and enough background to convince me your information is legit. If I believe you, I'll make all of this go away and I'll help with your brother's case."

Asher stared at him as if he'd lost his mind. "You can't promise to save her brother. No one can."

"I'm not saying that I can keep him from being executed. What I'm committing to is doing everything I can to dig into his case and, if I believe he could possibly be innocent as she claims, I'll *try* to prevent his execution."

"That's a lot of ifs," she grumbled.

"I'm not done yet. Everything I just said, I'll only do it if you can convince me that you're not playing some kind of twisted game, that your information is worth the paper it's printed on, before the police get here."

She looked around, panic making her heart pound faster, her head throb even worse. "I've been researching those murders for a long time. I can't possibly explain enough in ten minutes to—"

"Convince me, or go to jail."

Chapter Four

Callum looked up from his phone's screen as Faith and Asher entered the emergency room waiting area. Faith was pulling a small black duffel bag on wheels behind her. He waved to catch their attention and they hurried over.

There was only one empty seat on his side of the long, crowded room, right beside Callum. Asher waved Faith to the chair and leaned against a post a few feet away.

She nodded her thanks and set the bag beside her chair. "How's our unarmed abductor doing?"

Callum shook his head. "I still can't believe she pulled that stunt with an empty gun."

"She's lucky to be alive," Asher said. "That's for sure."

"Which brings me back to my question." Faith arched a brow at Callum. "How is she? Since she wouldn't let go of your hand at that ramshackle cottage and you rode in the ambulance with her, you must have some juicy details to share."

He rolled his eyes. "She grabbed my hand when

the police arrived because she was afraid I'd change my mind and have them arrest her. There's nothing juicy to share."

"If you say so."

Asher laughed, then coughed when Callum narrowed his eyes at him.

"Is she going to be okay?" Faith pressed. "Why aren't you in the emergency room with her?"

"Because I'm not her family." He didn't volunteer the fact that she had no family, no one outside of prison anyway. His guilt over hurting her had only been compounded when she told the triage nurse that she didn't have *anyone* to call to be with her. "She did sign a form, though, giving the doctor permission to provide me with updates once he's completed his examination."

He gestured toward the volunteer desk at the other end of the room where a middle-aged woman sat with an old-fashioned clipboard. "The last update I received confirmed she has a concussion but her vital signs are normal. When the CT scan comes back, if it looks good and she doesn't exhibit any neurological symptoms, aside from the headache, the doctor may let her leave rather than admit her."

Faith flipped her long hair over her shoulder. "Even if they release her today, she'll have to be checked every few hours to make sure she doesn't get worse or slip into a coma. That's what the doctor ordered for my sister when she had a concussion."

"Daphne had a concussion?" Asher asked. "She never told me that."

"She was ten, fell off her bicycle and wasn't wearing a helmet. And if my sister ever gets chummy enough with you to share details about her childhood, you're spending way too much time with her."

Asher grinned. "Thou shalt not date Faith's baby sister. Got it."

"Dang straight." She gave him a warning look, which only made him laugh.

Callum shook his head at them. "If the doctor releases her and wants her checked on throughout the night, we'll have to arrange for a home healthcare nurse."

"No need," Faith said. "I don't mind watching over her. The cabin she's renting isn't far from my place."

He frowned. "Why would you do that?"

"Why wouldn't I? She needs our help. Besides." She waved toward the duffel bag. "She delivered on her end of the deal you two made. All of the files were in the cabin right where she told us they'd be. The ones for her brother's case are in that bag. The others we put in Asher's car to take back to the office."

Asher cleared his throat, the look on his face immediately making Callum wary. "We may have stumbled on a little surprise while gathering all those folders. Did Raine happen to tell you that she's a lawyer?"

Callum groaned.

"She's not a *defense* attorney," Asher clarified, as Faith glanced back and forth between the two of them, clearly puzzled. "Not quite the lowest species on the legal food chain. She's employed by a firm near where you used to work, in Athens, Georgia. They specialize in business law. Seems like a catch-all for everything from mergers and acquisitions to human resource violations."

"That explains why she didn't seem knowledge-able about criminal law and death penalty cases. How did you find out about her firm? I wouldn't have thought you had time to research that deeply yet."

"I'd like to claim that I'm just that good, but instead I'll admit that her business card was stapled to the front of one of the folders she told us to get."

"Have you ascertained whether or not the information in those folders is worth me not pressing criminal charges and having to work with a lawyer on her brother's case?"

Faith held up her hands. "Hold it. Catch me up here. You have a problem with lawyers?"

Asher chuckled. "Massive understatement."

She frowned at him before looking at Callum again. "All of us, including you, respect and like the lawyers our company keeps on retainer. They've helped us countless times when we need legal muscle for our cases. And if I remember right, your friend in Athens, Brandon, is a prosecutor, isn't he?"

He shrugged, unwilling to concede the point.

"Come on, Callum. It's insulting that Asher knows this about you and I don't. Clue me in. Why are you so against an entire profession?"

"It's not a huge secret or anything. I've just... I had several bad experiences with lawyers when I was a police detective. I still bear the scars from my last major case at court. The defense attorney was un-scrupulous and twisted everything around to confuse the jury. Because of him, a murderer was set free."

"Major ouch. But automatically assuming Raine is a bad person because she's in the same profession as your nemesis isn't fair."

Callum stared at her in amazement. "Is it fair to assume she's a bad person because she held me at gunpoint and handcuffed me to a chair?"

Asher chuckled. "He's got you there, Faith."

"No. He doesn't. The gun wasn't loaded. She didn't actually hurt Callum. And she only threatened him because she loves her brother, believes he's innocent and is desperate to save his life. Love and family loy-alty drove her to do what she did. Otherwise, she'd never have crossed that line."

"Which line?" Asher asked. "The one where she kidnapped someone or the one where she tied them up?"

"Shut up, Asher."

He grinned.

"Back to Raine's research for our serial killer case. What did you find?" Callum asked.

Asher sobered. "An impressive amount of informa-tion, amazingly indexed and detailed. When she said she'd been investigating, she didn't mean as a hobby. She poured herself into it. I'd be hard-pressed to find a better documented case in my own archives."

"But will it help with our current investigation?"

He shrugged. "Until I review it more in-depth and corroborate her findings, I can't say for sure. But from what I've seen so far, if it pans out, yeah. It'll help. A lot. She may very well have found the key we need. As to the suspect she's zeroed in on, Pete Scoggin, Lance is already on his way to Athens, Georgia, to start surveillance on him while we build our own dossier. But even if Raine's wrong about the killer's identity, it looks promising that she's found several other murders that bear remarkable similarities to the murders we've already attributed to the serial killer we're trying to find."

"Meaning," Callum said, "if her information is reliable, then worst case, she's given us a lot more evidence to work with. Best case, she's solved a string of murders and all we have to do is tie up the loose ends."

"Pretty much."

Callum swore.

Faith lightly shoved him. "Stop being such a pessimist. This is good news."

"It's horrible news. It means I have to follow through on my part of the deal and work with her."

She shook her head in exasperation. "You never know. You may actually become friends."

"Not in this lifetime."

"You're impossible. When you come to her cabin to work on her brother's case, I may have to stick around so she at least has one person there who's friendly and supportive."

"You really plan on watching over her?"

"As long as she needs me, yes."

"If you want to spend your time getting chummy with her, feel free. Meanwhile, I'll be focusing on her brother's death row situation so I can resolve this as fast as possible and move on to my next cold case for UB."

The person sitting on Callum's right gave him an odd look, then got up and left the waiting room.

Asher chuckled and took the vacated seat. "If we raise our voices and talk more murder and mayhem, we could probably clear the whole waiting room."

Faith gave him an admonishing look. "This isn't a laughing matter. Poor Raine. Can you imagine a sister being under that kind of pressure, knowing she's the only hope her brother has at not being executed? Be nice to her, Callum. She's going through a lot." She held up her hands. "And don't lecture me again about what she put you through. You've survived far worse. And that was truly horrible that you counted down the minutes out loud until the police arrived, making her scramble to convince you about the information she had even though her head was hurting so much. You owe her an apology."

Asher's mouth dropped open in shock as he stared at her.

"Please tell me that was a joke," Callum said.

"Men." She crossed her arms. "In addition to the folders Asher and I have, we've got Raine's laptop. She gave me her password right before the EMTs loaded her into the ambulance, said she has more information on her brother's case on her computer. We'll take a look and see what we can find and print it out for you."

"Leave the laptop with me so I don't have to wait

for printouts. Speed is the name of the game with the clock ticking on her brother's case."

She arched a brow. "You sure you want to tackle her computer? You know how you are with electronics."

"Oh, good grief. Dumb luck and a few missteps here and there doesn't make me technologically challenged. And I'm not the only one who has problems using our ridiculously complicated videoconferencing system at the office."

Asher's eyes widened. "What about that time you managed to erase a suspect's confession while you were playing it back?"

Callum narrowed his eyes.

Asher laughed.

Faith shook her head at both of them. "I'll text you the password, Callum."

"I appreciate it. Asher, you said Lance is going to watch our potential suspect. I'm almost afraid to ask, but if we have a name and address, and as much information as you alluded to, can I assume that Raine performed physical surveillance on our would-be killer?"

Asher sobered. "No question. There are logs she kept that speak to his routine."

Callum fisted his hands on his knees. "I can see a lawyer, with no police background, performing surveillance on me by sitting in her car in the parking lot. I wouldn't have had a reason to notice her. But a murderer, a serial killer, is always on the hunt for his next victim. And on the watch for police who may be on to him. We need to consider that he may have noticed her at some point. For all we know, he could have decided to add her to his future victim list."

Faith turned pale. "He could be following her right now."

He nodded. "It's certainly possible. As soon as either of you hear back from Lance, give me an update. I'd feel a lot better about her security if our team locates him and we know he's nowhere near this place, or Raine's cabin she rented here."

"I'll let you know the minute Lance reports in," Asher told him.

"Thanks."

Faith motioned to Asher. "Go ahead and get Raine's laptop. It's under my book bag on the left side of your trunk."

"A please would be nice."

"Asher—"

"Okay, okay." He aimed a long-suffering look at Callum. "I'm not only Faith's chauffeur today, I'm her gopher."

Callum glanced back and forth between them. "Is there something I should know about the two of you? Something *juicy* the rest of our team might want to hear about?"

Horrified didn't begin to describe the expressions on their faces.

"My car's in the shop. I needed a ride." Faith managed to sound defensive and insulted at the same time. "And, please, seriously? Asher? And me? Not a chance, ever."

Asher frowned. "Hold on a minute. What's so bad about me?"

She arched a brow. "How much time do you have?"

Callum laughed and held up his hands. "All right, children. Continue your argument elsewhere." He motioned toward the volunteer working the desk, who was waving at him. "Looks like I'm being summoned." He stood and extended the duffel bag's handle so he could roll it behind him.

Asher frowned at Faith before heading toward the exit with long, angry strides.

She chuckled. "Be nice to Raine, Callum. Keep me updated on her medical status and let me know when to head over to her cabin."

"I'm always nice. And I'll keep you updated on Ms. Quintero as long as you keep me updated on your and Asher's budding relationship." He laughed when she made a rude gesture and hurried after Asher.

At the volunteer desk, he smiled at the bright red–haired woman in charge of updating visitors about their loved ones. "You have an update about Ms. Quintero?"

She added a check to one of the boxes on her clipboard and stood. "Doctor Bagnoli will meet you in privacy room three, just around the corner. I'll show you the way."

Callum had just settled into one of the plastic chairs in the windowless closet-like room when the doctor rapped on the door and stepped inside. Less than a minute later, Dr. Bagnoli was gone. And just like that, Callum was responsible for the health and well-being of a woman he barely knew. A woman he'd met under bizarre circumstances that had him wavering between wanting to help her and wanting to send her on her way.

Of course, that decision had already been made. A deal had been struck between them seconds before the police had arrived at the run-down cottage in the woods. As a result, he'd lied to the police. Something vague about misunderstandings. It was obvious they hadn't bought his fabrication. But Gatlinburg PD's excellent relationship and history with UB had smoothed the way for them to pretend they believed him and leave. Callum changing his mind wasn't an option now. There was no going back.

A few moments later, a nurse brought him into the busy part of the emergency room where patients were being treated and medical staff were scurrying around like ants in a thunderstorm. She pointed toward the curtained alcove where Raine was and hurried off to another patient.

When Callum was just a few feet away, he stopped, stunned and riddled with guilt again at how pitiful she looked. She was lying on her left side in the bed, her knees drawn up in a fetal position. Her eyes were closed, but she was frowning in her sleep. Since both of her hands were clutching her head, it didn't take a medical degree to conclude that she was in pain.

He immediately turned around and headed to the circular desk in the middle of the ER. A dozen nurses and doctors created a chaotic scene buzzing with activity. Some were talking to each other. A handful were on the phone. Several more were sitting at desktop computers or standing at the counter tapping on computer pads. They were all doing their best to ignore him.

He could understand their desire not to be interrupted, especially as overworked as they all appeared to be. But Raine needed pain medication and he wasn't going to back down until she got it.

The first person who had the misfortune of making eye contact with him became his target. Five minutes later, Raine was sleeping comfortably. Her frown was gone and she was no longer clutching her head.

"As soon as her doctor's release orders come through," another nurse told him, "I'll send someone in with a wheelchair so you can take her home. But don't be surprised if it takes a while. We're slammed around here. I'm not sure when the doctor will input the orders."

"Not my first time in a hospital. I know how slowly the wheels of bureaucracy can turn." He smiled to soften his words and thanked the nurse, who eagerly left, pulling the curtain closed behind him.

Callum settled into one of the ridiculously small chairs built for someone half his size and pulled the duffel bag beside him. After a quick glance at Raine to make sure she was still resting comfortably, he took out one of the thick folders and plopped it on his lap.

"All right, Ms. Quintero, attorney-at-law. Let's see what kind of a mess you've gotten me into."

Chapter Five

The sun was just barely beginning to rise over the mountains and peek into the glass rear wall of Raine's small rental cabin when a loud knock sounded on the front door. She hesitated, even though her spot at the kitchen island put her just a few feet from the entryway. Callum and fellow investigator Faith Lancaster were the only ones she expected to come by. But it seemed far too early in the morning for Callum to show up. Faith had stayed here overnight, checking on her per doctor's orders. But she'd headed down the mountain a few minutes ago to a café she swore had the best breakfast sandwiches for miles around. If she'd come back this quickly, something must have gone wrong—like maybe she forgot her wallet. She'd refused to let Raine pay, no matter how insistent she'd been.

At the hospital last night, after she awoke in the ER to find Callum sitting beside her bed, he too had refused to accept any compensation from her. She'd insisted that she could afford any fee or expenses he'd incur while helping her, and that she owed him a paint job for the scratches his SUV got while heading to the cottage. But he'd informed her that his boss, Grayson Prescott, had approved all expenses related to the work on her brother's case, because of the information she'd provided for their serial killer case. That had her feeling guilty, of course. Once her brother's…situation…was resolved, she'd circle back around to the discussion about reimbursing Unfinished Business, and Callum as well.

Another knock sounded, this one louder, as if her early morning visitor was growing impatient. It must be Callum after all. She couldn't imagine Faith acting impatiently. She'd treated Raine with nothing but understanding and kindness, far more than she deserved given the circumstances.

She scooted her chair back from the kitchen island and looked through the peephole in the door, unsurprised to see Callum staring back at her. She opened the door, and almost forgot how to breathe.

Callum in a suit had been…expected, normal, like most of the people she worked with on a daily basis. Callum in jeans, a snug black T-shirt and a black leather jacket that highlighted his dark hair and midnight blue eyes was anything but expected. Devastatingly handsome was one phrase that came to mind. The light stubble on his chiseled jaw, the golden tan, the…oh my goodness those shoulders, that flat stomach outlined by the formfitting T-shirt. How had she not realized how gorgeous he was until now?

He held up a laptop that she recognized as her own.

"You've been spying on me, Ms. Quintero." He brushed past her, pulling a rolling bag behind him.

Spying? Her stomach sank at the implications of that statement. He must have been exploring more than her brother's files on her computer. She slowly closed the door, mumbling, "Good morning to you too," as she followed him into the kitchen.

"Good morning," he surprised her by replying, his tone amused as he moved her coffee cup from the island to a countertop and sat in the same chair she'd just vacated. Without asking, he shoved the papers she'd been reviewing out of his way and set her laptop in their place.

Faith had better come back soon. Callum on top of a concussion was a combination she wasn't prepared to deal with before finishing her first coffee of the day. She'd like to think that if she hadn't banged her head she wouldn't feel so overwhelmed right now. But he'd been intimidating at the ramshackle cottage even before she'd gotten hurt.

"I need something for this headache." She started past him. His hand shot out and grabbed her arm, stopping her.

"When was your last pain pill? Is your headache worse than it was at the hospital?"

She shook her arm and he let go. But his piercing gaze pinned her in place just as well as his grip had.

Stop it, Raine. There's no reason to be flustered around this man.

Was she off-kilter because this was the first time she'd been *really* alone with him since the cottage?

Or because her head was pounding so hard now that she could barely think straight?

"Raine?" His brows drew together in a look of concern that had her more confused than before. "How bad is the headache? Any other neurological symptoms? Dizziness? Fainting? Maybe you should sit."

He started to rise from his chair as if to make her take his place, when her brain finally started working again.

"No, no. I'm fine, or I will be when I take the *prescribed* pain pill I'm *allowed* to take this morning."

His frown told her he wasn't sure he believed her. But he didn't try to stop her again.

She'd swear she felt the heat of his gaze following her as she got the prescription bottle from the cabinet and grabbed a bottled water from the refrigerator. Once she'd downed the pill, knowing relief would soon come for her throbbing head, she sat across from him at the island—with the coffee mug he'd moved earlier. After three deep sips of the caffeine-laden drink of the gods, she finally felt more in control and able to risk looking at him.

He was still staring at her with concern.

Her hand tightened around her coffee mug. "Why act so brusque at the door and then completely switch to being hyperconcerned for my welfare? Even Faith isn't worried anymore. I did fine last night and don't need babysitting at this point."

His eyes widened. "You're upset that I'm worried about you?"

"I'm confused. And aggravated. I don't know how

to read you, or…" Her face heated as he continued to stare at her. "Never mind. Like I said, I'm fine, or I will be once that pill and this coffee kick in. And before you ask again, no. I'm not having any other symptoms. Just brain fog and a headache that won't quit." She motioned toward the laptop in front of him. "I think I'd feel better if you confront me with whatever you found on my computer instead of pretending you care. Go on. Interrogate me. You accused me of spying on you."

He closed the laptop and set it aside, his mouth crooking up in a half smile. "Maybe I overreacted. After all, you did admit you'd been watching my routine when you pulled a gun on me. I shouldn't have been so surprised and angry when I saw the mounds of reports you wrote over the past week, cataloging my every move."

She grimaced. "Yes, well. I was prepping for our face-to-face meeting by learning everything I could about you. I wanted to be prepared. Turns out, I wasn't."

He crossed his forearms on top of the island. "Actually, I thought you were rather impressive in how you handled things. If you'd chosen a chair in that cottage that wasn't dry-rotted, I might still be handcuffed to it."

"Really?"

He chuckled. "No, not really. But you seem out of sorts this morning, even more than I'd have expected from your concussion. I was being nice."

She choked, then coughed. "This is you being nice?"

He shrugged, his smile firmly in place. "Let's start over. I'll forget about the stalking and kidnapping—for now—and that you're a lawyer. We've each made a deal with the devil, more or less, and we might as well make the best of it for however long we'll be working together. Or for however long it takes my team to prove, or disprove, your bribe—that research on the serial killer we're after."

His warning about her research had her feeling queasy. But it was the other part of his statement that really caught her attention.

"Deal with the devil? Because I'm a lawyer? Or because I held you at gunpoint?"

"Not sure I could choose one over the other."

She blinked again. "Wow. I don't even... What do you have against lawyers?"

"In the interest of forming a good working relationship and starting over, let's forget I said anything about your chosen profession." He held out his hand. "Hello. I'm Callum Wright, former police detective, currently an investigator for Unfinished Business, specializing in cold cases."

"Really? We're going to do this? Pretend the events of the past day—"

"Or weeks. Of stalking." He winked.

"We're pretending all of that never happened. I'm supposed to, what, ignore that you helped send my brother to death row? And in return you'll ignore that I *researched* you, not stalked, and that I'm a lawyer? So you can stomach being around me?" She arched a brow and crossed her arms.

He pulled his hand back, his smile fading. "New plan. We'll continue to nurse our grudges against each other but do our best to be civil so we can do what needs to be done."

She let out a frustrated breath. "That wasn't what I meant. I just—"

"When you started all of this, what was your goal? What did you hope I could accomplish? As I said, I was basically a gopher for Detective Farley on your brother's case. Before browsing the information last night that you provided, I could barely remember it. So why do you think I can help you? And how? Even if I had exculpatory evidence—which I don't— I have no pull with Georgia's governor to ask him for a pardon."

"It's not the governor we need to influence. In Georgia, he doesn't have that kind of power. The authority to grant pardons or commute death sentences to life in prison is held solely by Georgia's Board of Pardons and Paroles. And even though the governor appoints members to the board, the senate still has to approve them. Plus, they each serve on the board for seven years."

"Meaning the governor can't stack the board during his four-year term to have more sway over their actions."

She nodded. "Exactly. It's difficult, if not impossible, to sway the majority of the board to grant a stay of execution, or clemency. The only hope really is to present some kind of evidence that is so overwhelming that they can't ignore it."

"If you had that kind of evidence already, I imagine you wouldn't have gone to drastic measures to get my attention."

"No. I don't, and I wouldn't have. Obviously, I'm desperate at this point. My brother's set to be executed in a couple of weeks. Earlier you recommended that I hire a lawyer experienced with capital punishment cases. I have two, from two different firms. They've been doing everything they can to work through the appeals process and try to find new evidence that might exonerate Joey. Over the past month, they've been reinterviewing dozens of people the police originally spoke to, trying to find something, anything that would help. A while back, they even managed to get an audience before the board to argue for mercy. Nothing has worked so far and I have little faith that they're going to succeed. That's why I've taken a leave of absence from my job, so I could pursue any avenue I can think of to help him, before it's too late."

"Including risking being disbarred and going to prison yourself by holding someone at gunpoint and kidnapping them?"

Her face heated. "What I did to you isn't something I'm proud of. But my *innocent* brother is the only family I have left and he doesn't deserve to die for something he didn't do. In spite of what you may believe, there are limits to what lines I would cross to help him. With you, for example, the gun wasn't loaded. I was hoping to scare you into doing what I asked. Risking hurting you, or worse, wasn't something I could stomach. Thus, the gun was empty."

His jaw tightened. "Which reminds me, don't ever do that again. Only point a gun at someone if it's loaded and you're prepared to shoot. Otherwise, you're putting your own life at risk by bluffing. Someone calls that bluff and you could be killed."

"Careful, Callum. It almost sounds like you care."

"I do care, as one does for children or fools."

"You think I'm a fool?"

His mouth curved in a sardonic grin. "Well, you're definitely not a child."

She blinked, not sure how to take his comment and smile. On the one hand, he was insulting her by labeling her a fool. On the other, he was giving her a backhanded compliment, seemingly appreciating her as a woman. How could he seem so aggravating in one breath and ridiculously appealing in the next? She needed to get them back to safer ground. Even an argument was better than sitting across from this incredibly handsome man, half wishing she had the courage to bait him with a flirty response.

Clearing her throat, she said, "Regardless, what I'm after is your experience on cold cases in the hopes that you can find evidence to convince the board to at least stay my brother's execution. And the fact that you worked on his case, even in a minor role, would—I believe—have sway over getting the board to listen to you if you requested an audience with them to present new evidence."

He quietly considered that a moment, then shook his head. "You had to be a lawyer, huh?"

She frowned as he pulled out his phone. "I don't see what that has to do with—"

He held up a hand to stop her and pressed the phone to his ear. "Hey, Reid. Yes, it's Callum again. I'm calling about that possible favor we discussed last night. Yeah, looks like I'll be taking you up on it sooner than anticipated."

She crossed her arms and sat back as he spoke with this Reid person. What did Callum have against lawyers? Not that it really mattered. She wasn't going to apologize for her chosen profession. What mattered was helping her brother, Joey. If that meant tolerating a man who made her angry one minute and want to jump him the next, so be it. Her reactions to him made no sense. He confused and frustrated her. But that was something she'd have to deal with, somehow. Focusing on Joey's life being at stake was what she had to do, even if it meant being uncomfortable around Callum Wright for the next few weeks.

He ended the call and slid his phone into his back pants pocket. "How's that headache?"

She frowned, then pressed a hand to her temple. She'd completely forgotten about her headache. A reluctant smile curved her lips. "For the first time since I cracked my head against that hard floor, the pain is gone. Apparently fighting with you is some kind of cure."

"Is that what we're doing? Fighting?"

"What else would you call it?"

That sexy grin curved his lips again, but he simply shook his head. "I'll consider it my sacred duty to pick another fight if your headache returns." He pushed back from the island and stood. "I was going to sit here and discuss the information that I read about your brother's case. But, as you reminded me, the clock is ticking. We can save time by discussing it on the way to the other source I want to talk to. Grab your jacket."

"My jacket? Wait, we're leaving?"

"That's the plan. The sooner the better."

"But Faith, she went to get us breakfast—"

"I'll call her from my car and explain. If you don't mind a drive-through, I can get you something to eat on the way out of town."

"Drive-through is fine, but I don't—"

"Is that the hall closet, I'm guessing?" He motioned toward a door on the wall to the right of the front door.

She nodded.

He yanked open the door and grabbed a waist-length gray jacket. "Is this okay? I don't think it's cold enough today for the heavy coat."

"That's fine, thanks." She took the jacket he held out, then grabbed her purse from the small decorative table a few feet away. "Where are we going?"

After opening the front door, he motioned for her to precede him outside.

She shrugged into her jacket, but instead of doing as he wanted, she stood her ground. "I'm not leaving until you tell me where we're going. I may not agree that the time is well spent driving around in your SUV.

I can answer any questions you have, explain the case without us going to some other source to—"

"The man I just spoke to is a friend, someone I used to work with. We trade favors off and on and he currently owes me one, a big one. He's cutting through red tape to make that source I mentioned available. But only if we leave right now so we can arrive in the time frame he specified."

"Where? Who is this source you think can tell you more about my brother's case than I can?"

He arched a brow. "Your brother."

Chapter Six

Raine drew a shaky breath and forced herself to release her death grip on the passenger armrest in Callum's SUV. It had barely taken him four hours to make the drive from Gatlinburg, Tennessee, to the prison off Highway 36 in Jackson, Georgia. That included going through a drive-through for a couple of breakfast sandwiches. It would have taken her at least five, without the sandwiches.

He finally slowed and pulled into line behind a chase car and one of many white-and-red prison buses being escorted toward the gates. His driving had her reliving her childhood fear of roller coasters. At least now he couldn't speed. And they were no longer flying around dangerous curves through the mountains.

"Are you certain your friend has made it possible for us to see my brother? My next allowed visit with Joey isn't until the day of his... The last day of his incarceration. You're not even on his approved visitor list. Only immediate family, his lawyers or select media are normally allowed to see him."

"Reid is high up in the Georgia Department of Corrections. I don't really know what all he does for them, but he assured me he'll get an exception, and that I'll be on the list before we reach the checkpoint."

"He might not have had enough time to make that miracle happen. Does he realize how fast you drive?"

He grinned. "Sorry I made you nervous. I don't normally drive so crazy, but I didn't want us to miss this opportunity."

His easy apology, which seemed legit based on his tone, knocked her off-kilter again. Most men she knew would have been aggravated that she dared criticize their driving, even offhandedly. They certainly wouldn't have been amused, or apologized.

She glanced out the side window, toward the high chain-link fences topped with razor wire that surrounded the prison like a moat around a castle. "The red tape your friend will have to cut for us to see Joey spur of the moment like this is enormous. Visits are supposed to be planned and approved way in advance and they're severely limited or I'd be here much more often. This breaks every policy the prison has, especially for visiting death row inmates. Whatever you did to make him owe you a favor must have been something incredibly significant. Especially to visit on a Tuesday."

His smile faded. "It was. What's special about Tuesday? Reid didn't mention that as a potential problem when I spoke to him."

She wondered about the tension in him in regard

to the favor, but didn't feel it was appropriate to pry. "UDS prisoners, Under Death Sentence, are only allowed visitors on Saturdays, Sundays or state holidays. I've never been here on a Tuesday because of that. Tuesdays and Thursdays are intake days at Jackson Prison."

"Jackson Prison? That's not the name of—"

She waved her hand in the air. "That's what the prisoners, and family, call this place. It rolls off the tongue easier than Georgia Diagnostic and Classification Prison."

A hint of his smile returned. "So it does. I'm guessing intake day, judging by the name and all these buses and chase cars, is when they bring in the new prisoners."

"And ship some out, yes. This is the hub for all the prisons in Georgia. You go here first, from all around the state. Buses will be loading and unloading all day. The experts here evaluate each inmate's health, mental status, classify how dangerous they are, whether they need to be in PC, population levels at the other prisons—".

"PC. Protective custody?"

"Yes, to keep them safe from other inmates for various reasons."

"Like if a cop goes to prison?"

"That or, say, someone was convicted of murdering a child. I'm sure you already know that those types of convicts wouldn't last an hour in the general population. Once the prisoner has been assessed, they're assigned to their camp—their prison—and are shipped back out. It takes two to three weeks for each inmate to be processed and classified. But the bringing in of new men and shipping classified ones out to their new *homes* happens twice a week. Normally, for security reasons, they won't allow visitors to death row inmates on those days. Honestly, I'll be amazed if we reach the checkpoint and they allow us through. It's just not done."

His lack of concern was proven out as soon as the guards outside the crash fence checked both of their IDs. They were immediately waved forward.

When they stopped behind another gate, two men with mirrors extended on long poles checked under the SUV. Whether they were searching for bombs or some kind of contraband, she had no idea. But experience told her they'd do the same thing when she and Callum left, this time to ensure that a prisoner hadn't somehow managed to take a ride to freedom on their undercarriage.

They were directed where to park, in one of the few spots not close to one of the buses. They'd also been instructed not to unlock or open their doors until a guard arrived to escort them, which was the exact opposite of how most of her visits went. She was usually told not to sit in her car for any length of time. She was supposed to immediately exit and head to the building. But today, probably because it was Tuesday and their visit wasn't according to protocol, they had to wait. After setting her ID in the middle console, she stuffed her purse under the front seat.

"You don't want to take your purse inside?"

"Not allowed," she said. "They won't let you bring anything inside except your keys and ID. You should stow your phone, gun, change, whatever you've got in your pockets."

She didn't bother to admit she had her gun in her purse. He'd probably take it from her if he realized she was carrying it around. Faith had given it back to her after she'd promised never to pull it on anyone again unless her life was in danger. How Faith had managed to get it, Raine had no idea. But she was grateful. She might not like guns, or know much about them. But now that she'd bought one, she intended to keep it handy—especially if she had to go into some rough neighborhoods to try to get evidence to help her brother.

After emptying the change from his pockets and locking his wallet and pistol in the glove box, he sat back. There was no smile this time as he studied her. "How many times have you been through this routine?"

"Close to fifty, I'd guess. I visit every time I can get it approved. Death row inmates don't get the same monthly visits others get. Sometimes I'm allowed in once a quarter, other times only twice a year. It's ridiculous how stingy they are in allowing me to see him."

"I imagine the security is a nightmare for... I think you called them UDS prisoners earlier?"

She nodded.

"Security for them has to be especially rigorous. And the Georgia prison system is grossly understaffed these days. Some stats I've heard is that they have up to seventy percent of their job openings un-filled. There are several lawsuits and federal investigations pending because of it."

"Are you defending them to me? Seriously?" She crossed her arms in agitation.

He slowly shook his head, seeming sincere. "Not at all. What you're going through isn't something I could ever understand. But I can empathize with your frustration. I was making a lame attempt to reduce your frustration by explaining some of the logistical reasons behind those delays."

She lowered her arms. "Thank you, I guess. I mean, I appreciate that you were trying to reason things out. And I do understand the demands on the prison staff to allow the visits. But it seems to me that if someone is at the mercy of the state and is going to be murdered by the state, they should make every attempt at allowing that person's family to see them and try to bring comfort under such horrible circumstances."

"I imagine it's difficult to balance respect for the prisoner's rights and consideration of the victim, and their family. The state doesn't want it to look as if they're coddling prisoners. That would be an insult to the victims."

"Yes, well, I'd agree with that except that my brother is one of the victims. He's innocent."

His jaw tightened, punctuating his feelings on the matter, even after hearing her side of her brother's case during the ride here. But he respected her feelings enough not to argue the point any longer, for which she was grateful.

Although her brain agreed with everything he'd said, her heart rebelled because she didn't feel her brother should be lumped in with other convicts. He was innocent. And although she felt enormous empathy for the victim's family, having met with them herself many times over the years, it was a tight line to walk. The Claremonts deserved justice for their daughter, Alicia. But not at the expense of murdering a man who had nothing to do with her death.

"Looks like the cavalry is here to escort us to safety." Callum motioned toward a group of four burly guards heading toward his SUV.

As he reached for the door handle to get out, she put her hand on his shoulder. "Don't. Wait for them to direct you to open the door. Do one thing wrong, don't follow instructions in even the smallest way, and they'll immediately cancel the visit and send us packing. They run Jackson Prison like a military installation, with zero tolerance for mistakes."

She hated the bitterness in her voice but couldn't quite hide it. She'd been brutally punished by not being able to see her brother on no less than five visits because of some small or imagined infringement of the prison's strict rules. One time she'd forgotten she had cash in her pocket and that was enough to have her turned away when they searched her inside the visitor lobby. Sometimes she wondered if the guards had any feelings at all. Or maybe it was just their stubborn belief in "the system" that made them assume that her brother was truly guilty and therefore his sister must be trash like him.

A guard stopped outside each of their doors and motioned for them to get out. The other two guards stood with their backs to them, watching the "yard" with an intensity that had her beginning to feel something she rarely felt when coming to this place.

Fear.

She glanced around the crowded parking area, at the dozens of shackled prisoners standing in lines outside each bus. Normally when she arrived there weren't any convicts out here. There were so many today that she couldn't count them. And many were looking right at her, as if they'd lunge toward the SUV if given a chance, in a desperate bid for freedom.

"Follow the footprints, go, go, go," the lead guard told them.

She glanced down, a shiver of dread going through her when she realized they were being directed to follow the painted footprints on the asphalt that the prisoners normally walked when entering the prison. Knowing that Joey had once come in on those same buses, shackled head to toe like an animal, and that he'd taken this same path, had her beginning to shake. They were going to kill him, murder him, in less than two weeks. The next time she came here he'd be mere hours from death.

An arm settled around her shoulders. "It's okay," a kind, deep voice whispered. Callum's voice. "Lean on me. You can close your eyes if you want. Just put one foot in front of the other. I've got you."

She selfishly longed to do exactly that, lean on him, close her eyes. She wanted to put her fears, her frustrations, into this strong man's keeping and let him carry her burdens on his broad shoulders. But that wasn't fair to Joey. There was no one for him to lean on, no one to ease *his* burdens. And she wasn't a helpless damsel in distress. She'd been fighting the good fight in every way that she could since the day he'd been arrested, fifteen years ago. Giving up now wasn't an option. She had to be strong, see this through. For Joey.

Smiling her thanks, she gently moved his arm. Then she straightened her shoulders and followed in her condemned brother's footsteps.

Chapter Seven

Callum had half expected Raine to collapse by the car. But she'd surprised him, stiffening her back and marching toward the building as if her near panic attack had never happened.

Once inside, she'd demonstrated her knowledge of the procedures by directing Callum on filling out the visitor log. She'd provided her brother's inmate number from memory, as well as other required information. They both provided their IDs again, and one of the people manning the checkpoint area looked them up online to verify they were who they said they were and that they were preapproved for a visit. Raine explained to Callum that they were also confirming that the prisoner was available, not at court or in medical, that kind of thing. Information on the prisoner was written on a piece of paper and placed in the tray that would go through a metal detector, which was Raine's and his next step in the process.

The invasive procedures after that made TSA security requirements in airports seem pathetically inadequate. They were practically strip-searched, with all metal, shoes, belts, keys and anything else not required for modesty taken away. The metal detector didn't beep on either of them but they were still patted down then taken to separate "privacy rooms" for further searching.

Callum was told to untuck his shirt from his jeans and the male guard ran his hands around inside his waistband and even pulled his jeans away from him and peered down his underwear with a flashlight. Callum wondered what kind of embarrassment they were putting Raine through, but she didn't seem fazed when she met him back in the checkpoint area.

"How friendly did your guard get with you?" he whispered.

She smiled, for the first time in a long time. "I had to untuck, then lift my bra and shake my boobs to prove I didn't have anything tucked beneath them."

He stared at her, truly shocked. "They do that to all the women?"

"I assume so. Can't remember when they haven't done that to me. You get used to it, or as much as you can I guess."

One of the guards must have heard them and stared unflinchingly at Callum, as if to dare him to complain. Remembering Raine's warning about not following procedures to the letter, he didn't. But he sure wanted to. It bothered him to no end that she was treated as if she too was a criminal. He understood that the security measures were intended to keep everyone safe. Still, he didn't like it. Not at all.

The final step in the process was to get their hands

stamped. The ink wasn't viewable to the naked eye, but when a guard passed a UV light over them, the stamps glowed. Raine motioned him toward a doorway where yet another guard waited.

In spite of them having just had their hands scanned, he scanned them again and requested the slips of paper they'd been given earlier. The surprise on his face was evident when he read them, and rather than escort them to the visitation area where others had gone, he had them wait while he stepped down the hall and made a call using a landline phone on the wall.

Beside Callum, Raine sighed. Disappointment clouded her expression when she glanced up at him.

"I have a feeling your friend wasn't able to jump through all of those hoops after all," she said. "They aren't going to let us visit a death row inmate since it's not the right visitation day of the week. Joey also may have already used up his hour today, so that would be another reason for them not to let us see him."

"Used up his hour?"

"Death row inmates are locked in their cells twenty-three hours a day. They get one hour for showering or exercise or visitation. Joey didn't know we were coming, so he may have already used his free time."

Callum's respect for what Raine had suffered all these years was expanding exponentially. He honestly didn't think he'd have been able to take all of these onerous rules so well if their roles were reversed. Security was important. Punishment, or justice, made many of the rules necessary. But some of them, like being locked up twenty-three hours a day, seemed cruel. How was someone supposed to stay sane in an environment like that?

He supposed most people didn't care. And he was guilty of never considering the living conditions of death row inmates, until today. But what did treating people like animals say about those in charge of the treatment?

There had to be a better way to keep society safe from those who'd proven they couldn't be allowed to live amongst the public anymore. But Callum didn't have the answers to that quandary. Maybe no one did. The justice system was flawed in many ways. But he'd yet to see a better one anywhere else in the world.

Raine was still watching him, with worry wrinkling her brow.

He cleared his throat and tried to reassure her. "Don't give up yet. Reid's pretty resourceful. He wouldn't have told me he could get us in unless he was sure that he could. One of the things he told me last night was that, contrary to what you'd expect, the closer to the execution date you get the more likely they are to grant extra privileges."

"I've never heard that before. His lawyers didn't tell me that."

"I doubt the prison advertises it. They probably keep it on the hush-hush."

She smiled. It was a small one, but a smile nonetheless. "I can see them doing that, not wanting anyone to know that they don't follow their own authoritarian rules a hundred percent of the time."

The renewed look of hope on her face had him dreading what the guard might say when he returned. If their long drive and ensuing indignities turned out to be for nothing, Reid was going to owe Callum far more than one favor in the future.

A few moments later, the guard returned. Disapproval was heavy on his features as he waved them forward to the next gate. Callum thanked him and got a grunt in reply. He and Raine hurried down the hallway before the guard could change his mind about letting them through.

Another guard took them through another gate, its thick bars painted a cheery yellow in stark contrast to the drab off-white floors and gray cinder-block walls. They headed through a maze of hallways, sometimes coming upon prisoners in those same hallways. The guard with them would bark an order and the inmates immediately moved to the far side and faced the wall. They barely moved as Callum and Raine passed. He could see that military-style discipline she'd spoken about and was grateful for it. No telling what types of crimes those men had committed and the mayhem they'd do to Raine if allowed.

When they finally arrived at the death row portion of the prison, he was struck by how quiet it was. There were no chains rattling or prisoners shouting in the distance. No hum of activity from the sheer number of people in the building. It was as if they'd stepped from the bustling hive of a high school hallway into the tomb-like silence of a library. The only discernible noise was the muted hiss of ventilation equipment and the low tones of their guard's voice as he consulted with another guard who stood on the other side of a closed gate.

"I didn't expect it to be so quiet." Callum kept his voice low, much as he would in the library he'd compared death row to, or maybe a church.

She nodded, her gaze fixed on the guards, no doubt worried once again that they'd turn her and Callum back on the precipice of finally seeing her brother.

"In general, the UDS prisoners are quieter, better behaved than the rest of the population." She kept her voice low as well. "I've been told it's because many of them are still going through the appeals process. They don't want to do anything to jeopardize their chances, however small, of having their sentences overturned or commuted."

He nodded, once again feeling empathy he'd never expected to feel for the nameless, faceless men behind these walls. As a police detective, he'd participated in many cases that had resulted in death penalties for those who were found guilty. But this was his first time actually visiting a maximum security prison, let alone one with a death chamber on the grounds. It was much more difficult to feel satisfaction over a verdict when faced with the reality of that decision. Most, if not all, of the men locked in their cells just past the next gate would only leave this prison one way—in a body bag. It was a sobering reality.

A metallic clanging sounded, followed by the low electronic buzz of the gate rolling back. The earlier gates were opened with keys. This one, Callum realized, must have been unlocked remotely, by a control center that probably had eyes on them right now. There were cameras all over the building. This hallway was no exception. One of them was positioned in the top left corner over the growing opening.

Their guard motioned for them to approach. The second guard stared at them, eyes narrowed as he watched their every move.

"No talking," Raine whispered. "Follow my lead."

She handed the piece of paper she'd been given at check-in to the second guard. Callum did the same. The guard studied it a long moment, then sighed heavily and motioned for them to step through.

The other guard returned back down the hallway as the gate hummed, then began to slowly slide across the opening. As soon as it clanged shut, the three of them headed across a narrow common area devoid of people. There were three tables, and five TVs mounted high up on the walls, but they weren't turned on. Four hallways opened off the common area, presumably leading to the prisoners' cells.

It went against every protective instinct in Callum's body to walk behind Raine through an area designated for the worst of the worst that humanity had to offer. But she'd done this dozens of times before and had taken the lead. She knew the routine. And she'd already warned him not to do anything to break protocol. This close to their goal, he certainly wasn't going to cause any problems that might result in their visit being cut short. Raine would probably never forgive him. And he couldn't stomach the idea of robbing her of what was most likely one of her last chances to see her brother before he died.

At the far end of the room, rather than take them down one of the corridors of cells, the guard stopped them outside a metal door painted the same gray as the rest of the room. Using the radio on his belt, he identified himself and stated that he was escorting two visitors to the visitation area. He announced Callum's and Raine's names, as well as the prisoner's name and ID. Callum expected to hear an electronic buzz like with the gate. Instead, the guard shoved the radio back onto his utility belt and used a key to unlock the door.

A few moments later, Callum and Raine were alone inside the small visitation room with the door locked behind them. Their only instructions were to sit at the third of five windows and that the prisoner would be in shortly. They'd have approximately fifty minutes to talk to him using the old-fashioned telephone attached to the wall. Then the prisoner would be returned to his cell and the guard would escort them back to the general population area.

Raine hesitated in front of the lone metal stool attached to the floor in front of the window. She glanced up at Callum and he shook his head.

"Don't even try to get me to take the only seat," he said. "My mom taught me better manners than that."

She smiled a wobbly smile and sat.

Callum leaned against the partition to her right. "Will we both be able to hear him?"

"It's soundproof, I suppose to give the prisoners some kind of privacy when there are others here. You can only hear using the phone. We'll do our best to share it. If we can't hear well, we'll take turns talking to him."

"Fair enough."

She glanced at the analog clock on the wall above the glass, then watched the empty room beyond, her knuckles whitening where they gripped the laminate countertop in front of her.

Hoping to set her more at ease, Callum relied on the information he'd read last night on her laptop to make small talk. "Joey's older than you, right? Something like ten years?"

Her gaze stayed riveted on the only doorway in the other room as she waited for her brother to emerge.

"Twelve years. I was a senior in high school when he was arrested. Two years later, he was sent to death row."

And several years after that, both of her parents died. She'd had a rough time of it. And yet, from what he'd managed to find out about her through internet and law enforcement types of database searches, she was on track to be named a partner in the law firm where she worked. And she'd already become a wealthy woman in that short amount of time. Against all odds, she'd been hugely successful. Then she'd gambled it all on a foolhardy stunt, willing to give everything up on the slim chance that it would save her brother. Part of him thought she was nuts. But mostly, he was in awe of her family loyalty and the unconditional love that would make her risk it all.

"You do realize the odds of success, of getting his sentence commuted, are almost nonexistent, don't you?"

She finally looked away from the door and met his gaze. The haunted look in her eyes had his heart aching. No matter what she'd done to him on her foolhardy quest, she didn't deserve to suffer that kind of pain. No one did. He had to fist his hands at his sides to keep from reaching out to her and cradling her against his chest.

"I know the odds." Her voice was hollow, incredibly sad. "But until they stick a needle in his arm, I'm not giving up."

Unable to resist the urge to offer comfort in some small way, he took one of her hands in his and gently squeezed. "For your sake, I hope you're right and he's innocent. And that we can get him a stay of execution, if nothing else, then to have more time to fight for his release. But whatever happens, remember it's not your fault. You've done everything you can to help him. Don't blame yourself and wreck the rest of your life with could've, would've, should've."

Her eyes widened as she stared at their joined hands. But before she could say anything, movement on the other side of the glass had both of them turning. She tugged her hand free and pressed it against the glass as a man in a white jumpsuit and shackles on his wrists and ankles shuffled toward the window. A lone guard leaned against the wall about ten feet behind him, watching his every movement.

"What have they done to him?" she whispered brokenly as a tear slid down her cheek. "He looks awful."

The man on the other side of the glass was nothing like Callum had expected and barely resembled the mug shot Callum had viewed last night. He didn't know how much Joey Quintero had changed since Raine's last visit. But he looked as if he'd aged thirty years since his arrest.

Before entering death row, Joey had been tall and bulky, resembling a football linebacker. Now he was nearly bald, with grayish-white eyebrows and whiskers on his gaunt, lean face. Yellowing skin seemed to sag on his skeleton as he took his seat across from them. But it was the bleakness in his eyes that was the most shocking of all. There was no sign of recognition, no smile of greeting for his sister. And he barely glanced at Callum. This was the face of a man who'd lost everything and had no hope for a future of any kind.

Raine's hand shook as she picked up the phone. She held the receiver next to her ear, tilted away so that Callum could hear as well. He settled on his knees on the floor beside her stool and leaned in close to the phone.

When her brother sat, looking at her with no expression, she managed to muster an encouraging smile and motioned toward the phone on his side of the glass. He seemed to consider it a moment, as if he wasn't going to pick it up. But he finally did.

"Joey, it's so good to see you. Are you feeling okay? You look...tired."

The shackles on his wrists jangled as he rested his elbows on the counter and cradled the phone to his ear. "I live in a six-by-nine box twenty-three hours a day with no TV, no radio, nothing but an uncomfortable bed, a toilet, a sink and those sappy books you send me to pass the time. The guards turn on the lights and wake me up every half hour at night to make sure I haven't managed to escape or steal the executioner's fun by offing myself. What do you expect? Of course I'm tired. I haven't had a good night's sleep in over a decade. Why are you here, Raine? Get on with your life. Forget about me. You've wasted enough time on me as it is."

He raised the phone as if to hang up, but Raine frantically motioned for him to keep talking. His chest lifted in an obvious sigh and he held the phone to his ear again. "What?"

She swallowed, hard, her free hand still pressed against the glass as if she could feel him if she pressed hard enough. "Don't give up, Joey. There's still hope. The man with me is a private investigator and—"

"Another one? How many investigators have you hired over the years? My appeals are exhausted. There's nothing else you can do. Seriously, Raine. Please. Stop this. Let. Me. Go."

"I can't. Don't ask me to do that. We're going to

review the case, find some way to prove you're innocent."

He briefly closed his eyes as if in pain, then gave Callum his full attention for the first time. "Put him on the phone."

"He can hear you," she said. "We both can."

His cold gaze flicked to her. "Put him on the phone. Just him."

Callum wanted to slug the other man. His cruel indifference was clearly hurting his sister. He was going through a living hell in here—deserved or not. But that didn't justify him treating Raine this way.

She handed Callum the phone, her face pale and drawn as she clasped her hands in her lap.

Callum drew a bracing breath and focused on not shouting and upsetting Raine any more than she already was. "Mr. Quintero, I'm Callum Wright. I've agreed to take a fresh look at your case and see if we can get a stay of execution, clemency or a conversion of your sentence to life. Your sister has gone to incredible lengths, risked her career, even her own freedom, to convince me to help you. A smile or an I-love-you wouldn't hurt you one bit and it would sure as hell make her feel better."

Raine stared at him, wide-eyed, before quickly looking away.

Joey stared at Callum too. Then he started laughing.

Raine looked absolutely stricken.

Callum motioned to the guard behind Joey, then pointed at Raine. He nodded and spoke into his radio. Moments later, the door in the visitation room opened and another guard stepped in and waved for Raine to follow him.

She blinked and shook her head no.

"Raine." Callum's voice was low, just for her to hear. "Give me five minutes with your brother. Then come back in." When she started shaking her head again, he whispered, "You've trusted me this far. Don't stop now."

She stared at him, then glanced at her brother, obviously torn. Her lips quivered as if she was trying to hold back tears. Then she hurriedly left with the guard.

As soon as the door shut and locked behind them, Callum sat on the stool and faced the amused-looking man across from him.

"Joey. You don't mind if I call you Joey, do you?"

He shrugged, his smug smile still in place.

"Before your sister contacted me, I really hadn't bothered to look into the execution process in detail. Last night I did quite a bit of research on it. Has anyone ever shared with you exactly what's going to happen to you in thirteen days?"

His eyes narrowed and his smile slipped. But he didn't say anything.

"About twenty-four hours before they kill you, they move you to a holding cell called the death watch area. It's not a whole lot different than where you stay right now except it's a little bigger and has a shower. Upgrade. Cool, right?"

His eyelids lowered to half-mast as if he was

bored. But he was still holding the phone to his ear, still listening.

"You think you don't have much privacy now, wait until you're in that holding cell. A guard will sit right outside it the whole time monitoring your every move to make sure you don't, as you put it earlier, off yourself and cheat the executioner. Then there's the last meal. In Georgia, it's not some fancy takeout from your favorite restaurant. Other prisoners fix it here in the prison. Don't expect it to taste any better than what you eat every day."

Joey's mouth flattened, his knuckles whitening around the phone.

"If you haven't completely alienated your sister, the one person in this entire world who gives a damn about you, she might be allowed to visit you one last time—from outside of the cell. No touching. No final hug. The only ones who actually get to come into your cell are the warden and chaplain, and the guards of course."

Callum motioned toward Joey's white jumpsuit. "You'll probably wear those same clothes to your final appointment, except for one thing. You'll have to put on an adult diaper. That makes it easier for them to clean up the mess when your bowels empty the moment you die."

Joey swore, a litany of curse words and phrases that questioned Callum's parentage and accused him of several disgusting fetishes.

Callum responded the way Joey had to Raine.

He laughed.

"You don't want to miss this last part," Callum said. "Once they take you to the execution chamber, they strap you to a table, arms spread and tied down, completely vulnerable. That makes it easy for them to shove that needle in your arm. Then they open the curtain. One-way glass. They can see you but you can't see them. And you know who will be out there? Watching? Praying for your soul?"

He leaned up close to the glass. "No one. That is, unless you apologize and fix the hurt you just did to your sister. If you don't, I guarantee she won't be there for you. I'll make sure of it. I refuse to let you hurt her again."

"What the hell do you want from me?" Joey demanded, spittle running down his mouth, his earlier smugness replaced with anger and a flash of fear.

"You want to know how it ends, right? They'll let you say your last words. But, again, no one who cares will be there to hear them. So it really doesn't matter what you say. It's just fodder for the twenty-four-hour news cycle, until the next story comes along and they completely forget you."

Joey's nostrils flared, the whites of his eyes showing as his Adam's apple bobbed in this throat. He was trying to play it cool, pretend nothing Callum was saying mattered. But it clearly did.

Callum continued his attack, firing with both barrels. "They'll pump you full of sodium thiopental to supposedly put you to sleep." He shrugged. "Who really knows what you'll be aware of? What you'll hear. What you'll feel. The second drug is pancuronium bromide. It paralyzes your diaphragm, your lungs, so you can't breathe."

Joey's face turned white. His lips lost their color.

"The last drug they pump into you is potassium chloride. It stops the heart. Assuming everything goes as planned, maybe you won't feel pain. Maybe you will. The only thing for sure is you'll be dead. As dead as Alicia Claremont, the young woman you killed fifteen years ago. Death is never a pretty thing. But imagine dying alone, with only the guards and executioner to keep you company instead of knowing that someone you love, and who loves you, is out there, praying for your soul."

Joey winced and looked away, clearly shaken.

Callum went in for the kill. "If you die with things between you and your sister the way they are now, her last memories of you will erode all the good ones from the past, from when you grew up together and cared about each other. She'll forever resent how you treated her when she's done nothing but sacrifice for you for the past fifteen years. You think you've suffered in here? Think about her, how she's put her hopes and dreams for her life on hold so she can focus on you and trying to get you free. Sure, she made herself a good career, and money. But why do you think she did that? So she could fund your defense. So she could give you the best possible chance at a future, at a life. And you re-paid her by being a complete and utter jerk, to put it mildly."

Joey glared at him, red dots of color brightening his pale cheeks. "Don't you get it, dude? I love my sister. I know what she's sacrificed for me. She should be married with babies by now and instead she spends all her free time working on my case." He swore. "I was doing her a favor, trying to make her want to forget me. I don't want her grieving me and ruining even more of her life when I'm gone."

Callum shook his head. "She's going to grieve for you whether you leave bad memories in her heart or good ones. You can't turn off her emotions like a switch. If she didn't care about you, deeply, she wouldn't have stuck with you all these years. One conversation isn't going to somehow keep her from being hurt. The way you spoke to her just piles more hurt on what she's going to feel if we don't succeed in getting your sentence overturned."

"What the hell am I supposed to do then?" Joey demanded.

"Be a decent human being. Apologize, tell her that you're having a bad day and shouldn't have taken it out on her. Do whatever it takes to make her feel better, or I'm off this case. And, believe me, no one else is jumping up and down wanting to help. You want to live? Potentially have a chance at some kind of future, possibly even your freedom? Then you have to do two things. One, convince me you didn't kill Ms. Claremont. Two, grovel to your sister and repair the damage you did earlier."

Joey's eyes widened. "You like her, don't you? That's what this is all about. You're interested in her so you don't want her upset. That's the whole freaking reason you're here, to get into my sister's pants."

"Goodbye, Joey." Callum stood and hung up the phone.

Joey slammed his fist against the glass, gesturing wildly toward the phone and obviously yelling even though Callum couldn't hear him.

The guard behind him pushed away from the wall and said something.

Joey held up his hand, his manner turning placating until the guard positioned himself back against the wall. A look of desperation crossed Joey's face as he urgently motioned toward Callum's phone.

Callum really did want to leave. The clock above the phone showed they had only thirty more minutes for the visit. From what he'd read of this scumbag's case last night, he doubted there was anything Joey could say that could convince him he wasn't the murderer the court believed him to be.

And he really couldn't stomach how Joey had treated Raine.

But as Joey continued to gesture toward the phone, Callum realized he couldn't just walk out and leave it this way. Not for the man on the other side of the glass, but for the woman on the other side of the door. Coming here had given him a new perspective on what she had suffered for years and years. And it had pretty much taken away the sting, and embarrassment, of having been surprised by her at gunpoint. He could understand her desperation now, at how she felt she was without other options. And his respect for her, for the sacrifices she'd made, and had almost made, to help her brother meant Callum couldn't just walk out and crush her hopes at this point. So, for Raine, Callum sat and picked up the phone.

Mimicking Joey's earlier attitude, he demanded, "What?"

"You're cold, dude. Stone-cold."

Callum lifted the phone toward the receiver again.

Joey frantically waved at him.

Callum pressed the phone back to his ear. And waited.

"Okay, okay. I'm sorry, all right? I was out of line when I said that stuff about you. And I don't want to die, not if there's a chance you can stop it and get me off death row."

"And?"

His throat bobbed again as he swallowed. "And I get what you're saying about Raine. I didn't really want to hurt her. I was trying to help, in my own stupid way. I thought it would be easier on her if she was mad at me at the end. She's bullheaded. Anyone else would have given up on me long ago. But she refuses to stop. I need her to be okay when I'm gone. I just... I don't know how to get her to let go and be okay."

"Did you kill Alicia Claremont?"

He blinked. "No. No, I didn't."

"But you confessed."

He rolled his eyes. "They interrogated me for twenty hours straight. I would have told them I assassinated the pope if it would make them let me lie down and get some sleep. I didn't kill no one, okay?"

Callum stared into the other man's eyes. Usually he could read people pretty well. But he honestly wasn't sure what he saw this time. Joey could be innocent, as Raine believed. Or he could be the savage killer he'd been convicted of being.

"I'll lay it out for you, Joey. I work for a cold case company, Unfinished Business. We have a large team of some of the best investigators in the country, along with our own private lab, just for starters. If anyone can find reasonable doubt this late in the game and convince the board to stay your execution, it's UB. But we're not lifting a single finger on your behalf until you've done one thing."

His fingers curled around the phone. "Anything, man. Name it."

"When your sister comes back in here, you're going to do whatever it takes to make her smile again. Fix the damage you did or you can kiss your last chance at justice, and life, goodbye."

Chapter Eight

Raine glanced back and forth between her brother
on the other side of the glass and Callum, who was
standing after insisting once again she take the only
stool in the little partition. But they weren't sharing the phone this time. Instead, Callum was firing
questions at her brother, trying to get as much information as possible before their visit ended. And although her brother had been unbelievably sweet and
apologetic to her when she'd returned, his disposition
had turned sullen and angry beneath the barrage of
questions that Callum was asking.

If it was anyone else, at any other time, she'd have
demanded he leave her brother alone. But this was
what she'd wanted, what she'd risked everything to
get—a top-notch investigator doing everything he
could in an extremely limited time frame to try to
save her brother's life. For that reason alone, she
clasped her hands together and forced herself not
to intervene.

"Her name was Alicia Claremont," Callum snapped
into the phone. "Quit calling her *that woman*. Have

some respect for the victim. If we're able to get you a hearing, you need to adopt a better attitude. Otherwise, you'll alienate the board and they won't bother to help you, regardless of what kind of evidence we're able to assemble."

Joey didn't exactly appear contrite as he responded. But whatever he said seemed to placate Callum, to some extent. He fired off more questions about the case, in rapid succession, barely giving her brother time to respond to each one. It was likely because the clock above the glass kept ticking away their remaining few minutes. But she also suspected it was Callum's interview style, at least in this situation, that catered to her brother's personality. The rapid-fire questions gave Joey no time to be sarcastic or flippant as he often could be. It forced him to let down his guard and say the first thing that came to mind, instead of trying to paint himself a certain way or avoid the uncomfortable questions. She admired Callum's skill and hoped he was getting what he needed in order to make his decision on whether or not to continue trying to help him. If Joey didn't convince Callum that he at least *could* be innocent, then Callum would drop his investigation.

Please, God, she silently prayed. *Help Joey convince Callum that he's not a murderer. If Callum doesn't help him, I don't know what else to do.*

Twenty minutes later, after a tearful goodbye to her brother, she was in Callum's SUV as he drove them outside the last of the prison gates. As always, when leaving her only sibling, there was a mixture of relief and grief inside her. Being inside those gray walls was overwhelmingly stressful. But knowing that her brother, unlike her, couldn't walk out, maybe never would, had her fighting back tears.

As if he understood the turmoil going on inside her, Callum remained silent. Occasionally, he glanced over at her, as if concerned. But he didn't intrude, didn't push. He gave her the space she needed. And for that, she was grateful.

They were well on their way back to Gatlinburg before she finally had her emotions under control enough to say anything.

She cleared her throat, and straightened in her seat. "What did you say to my brother?"

He glanced at her, before putting on his blinker and passing a slow-moving car. "I said a lot of things."

"I mean when you two were alone. After that, when I came back into the visitation room, he'd snapped back to the brother I remember. How did you make that happen?"

He shrugged. "I reasoned with him."

She clenched her hands in her lap. "I love my brother, more than you'll probably ever understand. But I also know him better than anyone. He deals with stress and fear by becoming belligerent and rude. Somehow you managed to make him remember his manners and give me a rare glimpse of the way he used to be, before…before the police pressured him into that false confession and destroyed his life. Whatever you did, thank you. Seriously. That was a rare gift, to see him once more the way he once was. Thank you."

"I'm glad I was able to help."

"You did. You really did. And I'm hopeful that you'll continue helping. Did you get the information that you needed to make your decision?"

"Are you asking if I think he's not guilty of murder?"

"Yes."

He passed another car before answering. "Honestly, he didn't tell me anything that made me think he'd been railroaded into a conviction. He wasn't on drugs or drunk when he confessed. He readily admits that. And he doesn't have an alibi."

"Correction, he has an alibi. Being home alone isn't a crime."

"No. It isn't. But if it can't be corroborated by some other means, it's useless as a defense."

"He'd never even met Alicia. Why would he kill her?"

"One of his friends said he saw Joey and Alicia get into Joey's truck outside a bar the night she was killed."

She rolled her eyes. "Friend? We're talking about Randy Hagen? That guy would do anything for his fifteen minutes of fame. He and Joey weren't friends anymore, hadn't been for a while. Randy had grudges against my brother. I don't believe anything he said on the witness stand. Neither do my brother's lawyers. They talked to him again a few days ago trying to get him to recant. The jerk refuses."

"Maybe because he was telling the truth. His testimony matched your brother's confession."

"I told you—"

"The confession was coerced, says everyone who's ever confessed."

"It was. The detective who interviewed him—your former boss, Farley—had just finished interviewing Randy. Then he took that information into the interview of my brother and lo and behold my brother's so-called confession matched."

He shrugged noncommittally.

She crossed her arms in frustration. "Are you going to help him or not?"

He was silent so long that she was convinced he was trying to figure out how to let her down. No doubt he'd made up his mind about Joey's guilt before they even entered the prison. Her brother's demeanor hadn't helped. And his answers to Callum's questions must not have done him any favors.

What was she going to do now? Tomorrow would mark twelve days until his execution. The two new lawyers Raine had recently hired hadn't made any real progress. Callum was her last resort. Was she really at the point of having to give up? Was there nothing else she could do to save the life of the only family member she had left?

She looked out the window just as they passed a highway sign. She frowned and noted another sign coming up ahead. "We're on Highway 36? That's not the way to Atlanta. You know a faster way to Gatlinburg?"

He surprised her by smiling. "Not hardly. But it's the fastest way to Athens."

She jerked around in her seat, afraid to hope. "Athens? Why?"

"Now who's pretending to be obtuse? It's the scene of the crime, the best way for me to get the lay of the land, to see what the killer saw, make sense of some of the reports I read and compare them to what your brother said today."

"Does that mean you're—"

"I'm going to work your brother's case, at least until I find out he's guilty. The second I'm convinced of his guilt, I'm off the case."

She impulsively took off her seat belt and planted a kiss on his cheek. "Since he's not guilty, that's not a worry. Thank you, Callum. Thank you, thank you, thank you. This means everything to me."

He chuckled and gently pushed her back. "It would mean everything to *me* if you put your seat belt on. Accidents are never planned and I don't want you flying through the windshield. I'm already going to have to get a new paint job. Replacing a broken windshield on top of that would be a major headache."

She laughed and clicked her seat belt into place. "Nice to know you care. About your car, that is."

"I do, you know." He glanced at her, his smile gone, his gaze locked onto her with an intensity that stole her breath. "I care what happens to you. I respect you, admire your courage and willingness to give up everything you've worked for in order to help your family. That kind of loyalty is rare, inspiring."

She blinked, her face growing warm before he finally looked back at the road. "Thank you. I appreciate that. I, ah, admire you as well, to be completely honest here. Even knowing that you worked on my brother's original case, even if it was only running errands for the lead detective, I wouldn't have come to you for help except that I read about your successes as a detective later in your career. And, of course, for Unfinished Business. That was the final factor that made me decide to—"

"Kidnap me at gunpoint?" he teased.

Her face heated even more. "I'm never going to live that down, am I?"

His grin widened. "Probably not."

"Well, I guess it was worth it if it made you decide to work the case. Because I'm so courageous, of course. And loyal."

"There's that, yes. But I'm in this for my own selfish reasons as well. I don't know that I'd have bothered even going to the prison or reading the files if it wasn't for the information you gave us on the serial killer we've been trying to catch. Everyone working that investigation is digging into your research. We're pinning our hopes that it's the key to finally stopping this killer, before he claims another victim."

Her stomach lurched as she forced a smile. Once he focused on the road again, she focused on the scenery passing by her window. What had he said exactly? That everyone was pinning their hopes on the information she'd provided? Were they all working that angle instead of the leads they were following before she came along?

Nausea roiled in her stomach. Her plan had worked, a little too well. She clenched her hands in her lap and drew deep, even breaths to stave off the panic rising inside her.

Sweet Lord. What have I done?

Chapter Nine

The residential neighborhood that Callum pulled into that evening, just outside of Athens, Georgia, was what he supposed would be called transitional, or up-and-coming. Most of the homes appeared to be from a bygone era, built long before Callum was born, maybe even before his parents were born. Largely single-story wooden structures, they were on the small side and boasted cracked and peeling paint, some with their siding sagging or even missing in places. But every fourth or fifth house was completely different, usually two-story, big and modern. People were buying up the older homes and tearing them down, replacing them with the boxy, cookie-cutter look found in so many other subdivisions. And the reason for them buying out here was obvious.

The enormous lots.

This neighborhood was originally built in an era when large lots were the norm. Graceful oak trees and gently rolling yards with occasional flower beds bursting with color gave it a homey feel, a welcoming atmosphere. There was plenty of land on each lot to allow for a much larger home to be built. And it still left room for large backyards with established trees to provide beauty and shade. The newer homes on lots this size didn't exist deeper into the city. Or, if they did, they'd be double the price.

"Nice, isn't it?" Beside him, Raine had a serene smile on her face as she looked out the window, obviously pleased with what she was seeing.

When he realized which homes she was admiring, he couldn't help feeling surprised.

"You like the old ones? Not the new builds?"

"Well, yeah. Don't you? The new ones look like boxes." She motioned toward the window. "These are unique, charming. I mean, sure, they need repairs. But they're different, special, a piece of history to be appreciated."

"And yet you live in a mansion in a development where the houses are so close together that you could jump from roof to roof."

She frowned. "First, it's not a mansion. Second, how would you know about my house?"

"I'm an investigator."

"And you felt you needed to investigate me?"

"Like you did me?"

She grimaced. "Fair enough. I guess." She motioned toward the nearest house again. "If I wasn't bucking for a partnership in a law firm with an image to maintain, I could see myself living here. Absolutely. Then again, my Porsche would be out in the elements with only a carport to protect it. Maybe I couldn't live in one of these after all."

"Porsche. You actually drive one of those things?"

"It's a sweet ride. My gift to myself after a particularly lucrative case. Why do you look so surprised?"

He shrugged. "I guess maybe because all I've seen you in so far is jeans. I'd have guessed you drove a crossover, a small SUV or something like that."

"Maybe I should rethink your abilities as a detective. My other car, the one I drive to the grocery store and things like that, is a truck."

He laughed. "That's a surprise. Regular or four-wheel drive?"

"Four-wheel. Duh."

"Red?"

"Of course."

"Nice. That's what I'd call a sweet ride."

"And yet you drive an SUV."

He grinned. "It's my work car, like your Porsche's yours. My regular ride is a four-by-four. Red."

She laughed and they exchanged a fist bump. "We're more alike than either of us realized."

"I suppose we are. But if I'm going to get anything useful to help me get my bearings on this case before the sun goes down, we need to get busy." He popped his door open.

"Busy doing what?" she asked. "If you wanted to see the crime scene, the Claremonts live one street over."

"Like I said earlier, I want to get the lay of the land." He hopped out and went to the rear of the SUV and opened the hatchback. When Raine joined him, he'd already gotten out his drone and was readying it for takeoff.

"Wow. Way fancier than the one I have," she said.

"You use a drone for work?"

"No. I'm a regular, boring business lawyer. No use for a drone for that. Mine's for weekends to, as you said, get the lay of the land. I scope out places to take pictures, and get some pretty good ones with the drone itself too."

"Pictures."

"Photography. Nature, landscapes, that sort of thing. It's what I wanted to do before my parents talked me into getting a *real* job. I was going to major in photography at college, try to sell pictures to magazines, stuff like that. But I guess it's a good thing that they talked me out of it. Odds are I would have had to work an extra job just to pay the rent. That wouldn't have provided the money I've needed to fund my brother's defense." She cleared her throat, her earlier enthusiasm fading. "Not that it's done him any good."

He stepped back and sent the drone airborne. "We've got thirteen days to find reasonable doubt. Don't give up now."

She nodded but didn't look convinced. He couldn't blame her. Joey's various lawyers had been trying for years to have his conviction overturned, to get him a new trial. Bringing Callum in to save the day was like bringing in a pinch hitter at the bottom of the ninth with two outs in a baseball game. The odds of success were low. But they weren't zero. They had a chance, but only if Joey was truly innocent. And so far, Callum had seen nothing to convince him of that.

"What was your dream, career-wise, when you were younger?" She stood beside him, watching the controller's screen as he directed the drone higher to show him a better view of the neighborhood, including its relation to nearby highways and other local roads.

"My mom told me I've wanted to be a policeman since I was old enough to talk."

"Really? Why? I mean, not that it's a bad thing, of course. It's admirable. Honestly. But what would make a child, a two- or three-year-old, say they wanted to be a cop? And then you being so focused through life that you ended up actually doing it?"

He shrugged, noting how the homes deeper inside the subdivision were on even larger lots, with more trees, overgrown bushes. Lots of places for bad guys to hide. "I suppose because it runs in the family. I grew up around uniforms, guns. My dad was a military policeman. Mom worked the phone lines, a 911 operator. That's how they met. My grandfather on my dad's side was the chief of police in the small town where he grew up, Mayfield, Kentucky."

"No wonder you're inclined to believe in my brother's guilt. I'm surprised you showed mercy and didn't have me arrested after the stunt I pulled."

He smiled. "Yeah, well, like I said. Selfish reasons." What he wouldn't tell her was that in addition to wanting the information she had that might help with UB's current serial killer investigation, he'd also been curious about her.

She was a looker, no denying that. But it was her determination, her willingness to risk it all for her brother that had him wanting to know more about her. In spite of his seemingly illustrious family history in law enforcement, he wasn't close to them. That whole family loyalty thing was nonexistent in the Wright household, particularly with his father. It was the reason he hadn't seen him or the rest of his family since he was eighteen and had left to go to college—on his own dime, working two jobs to pay for it. His parents could have easily footed the bill if they'd wanted. They had for his sister's education.

"There's the Claremont house." She pointed to a white older home on his screen. "That two-story addition on the back is new, built in the last six months."

"How would you know that?"

"Because the last time I visited them, it wasn't there."

He glanced at her, surprised, before he looked back at the screen and sent the drone soaring over the Claremont house. "You've visited the parents of the woman your brother was convicted of murdering?"

She edged away from him, as if suddenly uncomfortable being so close. "It wasn't my idea. It's not like I showed up on their doorstep one day. That would have been wildly inappropriate, given the situation. But I couldn't ignore what had happened. Yes, I believe my brother's innocent. I know he is, with all my heart. But Alicia's parents didn't grow up with Joey. They have no reason not to trust and believe what the police told them. In their hearts, Joey's the enemy, the one who ripped their lives apart. But I'm his sister, his family. It was my responsibility to reach out to them and apologize on my family's behalf. I sent a card, and a letter, through one of Joey's attorneys, expressing my heartfelt condolences on their terrible loss. I told them I sincerely believed the killer was still out there, but that I also wanted them to know I understand why they feel my brother hurt her, and that I'm sorry for the pain they've suffered."

She shrugged. "Lame, I know. But I felt I had to say something."

Raine had surprised him again. She was turning out to be very different from what he'd expected. In spite of her being a lawyer, and the sister of a convicted felon, he was liking her more and more. That was the biggest surprise of all.

"How did they react to the letter?" He finished reviewing the land surrounding the house and sent the drone to explore the neighboring yards, looking for escape routes, ways to sneak onto the property without being seen.

"Instead of sending a reply through the lawyer, or ignoring me altogether, they called me at work."

"You're kidding."

"Nope. I almost had a heart attack, burst into tears when I answered the phone. My assistant thought they were potential clients, didn't recognize the name. When Mr. Claremont introduced himself, it was like being hit by a truck." She shook her head, let out a ragged breath. "He was so sweet, so kind and understanding. They both were, are. They wanted me to come see them at the house."

"When was this?"

"A week after Joey was convicted."

"Amazing. How did that go? I'm guessing pretty well if you see them regularly, enough to know their home renovations hadn't been done six months ago."

"I see them once or twice a year. But the first visit wasn't until several months after they called me. Sending them a letter is one thing. Actually seeing them in person, sitting across from them in the same house where their daughter once lived and knowing that they believed Joey killed her wasn't something I was prepared to do. It took a while to get the courage to see them. When I did, they were incredible. They wanted me to know they didn't hold Joey's actions against me, that they didn't blame me for trying to defend him because he was my brother. They understood me, like no one else ever has. Well, until now, I guess. You seem to have forgiven me for my actions, because you understand family loyalty."

"More like I appreciate the *concept* of family loyalty, not having experienced it myself."

"What do you mean?"

He sighed and steered the drone back toward them. "That's a conversation for another time. Maybe."

She was quiet until he'd stowed the drone in his vehicle and shut the back hatch.

"Now that you've seen where it all happened,

what's next?" she asked. "It's a long drive from here to Gatlinburg, and it's already getting dark. We could go into town for dinner and stay at my place tonight, head out in the morning."

"I appreciate the offer. Sounds better than crashing at a hotel tonight. But I'm not finished here. I understand the surroundings better, but not the crime scene itself."

Her gaze shot to his. "You actually want to go inside their home? See where Alicia was…where she was killed?"

"I'd planned on contacting the Claremonts tomorrow, seeing whether they'd let me come to the house, without you, out of respect for them. But now that I know they wouldn't be upset if you came too, we might as well save time by visiting them now. There's a car in their driveway. Someone's home."

Her eyes widened, her expression panicky. Had she made up that story about her letter to them, and their phone call? Maybe she'd fabricated everything to make him feel more empathetic toward her, and vicariously toward Joey. The idea that she'd lie about something like that had him tensing and wondering what else she'd lied about. She was a lawyer, after all. He should have known better than to trust her.

"If you'd rather not go with me—"

"No, no," she interrupted. "I'd love to see them. I'm just—"

"Worried I'll discover you've never really met them?"

Her mouth dropped open, then her face reddened

as she snapped her mouth shut. She cleared her throat as if struggling to speak. "You think I lied?"

"Did you?"

She swore beneath her breath. "I guess we'll find out, assuming they'll want to see you. My hesitancy is because I don't want them hurt. I don't want you dredging up awful memories and causing them pain."

"That's for them to decide. Not you."

"Then I guess we should head over there. But I'm going in first, alone, to pave the way and make sure they'll be okay." She marched to the passenger side of the Lexus and hopped in.

"The hell with that," he muttered to himself, as he headed toward the driver's door. "I'll go in first so I can see their reaction to *you*."

Chapter Ten

Raine squeezed Mrs. Claremont's hands in hers, then smiled up at Mr. Claremont just inside their foyer. "Please don't feel you have to leave. I can sit with you while Mr. Wright does a walk-through. We'll be in and out in no time. You won't have to answer any questions."

She ignored Callum behind her. No doubt he was fuming that he wouldn't get a chance to talk to them about Alicia. But these kind people had suffered too much pain already. Raine wasn't going to stand for him interrogating them, even if it was to help Joey.

Mr. Claremont patted her shoulder. "You two take as long as you need. You can call me when we should come back. We understand how important this is to you. And we want you at peace, knowing you explored every option, that you did everything you could for your loved one. We'd do the same if the situation was reversed."

Raine smiled her gratitude through threatening tears. "You've both always been so kind to me, so understanding. I don't know how you do it."

Mrs. Claremont squeezed Raine's hands before letting go. "You act as if we get nothing in return. Talking to you on the phone, seeing you, getting cards, flowers, those things give us something to look forward to in a house that's far too quiet these days. You keep Alicia alive for us. You make us feel alive. As far as we're concerned, you're our second daughter. We love you, Raine."

"I love you too," she whispered brokenly, and hugged them both.

As they stepped out the door, Mrs. Claremont turned back with one last smile. "It will be okay, Raine. You'll get through this. Whatever happens, we're here for you."

She forced a smile and watched them drive away, then slowly shut the door.

"You're shaking." Callum's arm settled around her waist, as if he was afraid she would pass out. "Come on. Sit on the couch."

Being treated as if she was helpless normally would have made her snap back in resentment. She'd worked too long and too hard to make it in a man's world to be treated like a stereotypical weak female. But she did need to sit down. And she was so dang tired of having to be strong all the time. Plus, he was right. She was shaking, and she wasn't sure how much longer her legs were going to hold out.

Her face flaming, she let him lead her to the couch where she gratefully sat. Too embarrassed to look at him, she rested her elbows on her thighs and held her head while she closed her eyes.

"Go ahead," she said. "Look around the house for whatever you think you'll find fifteen years after the murder. I just need a minute."

"The house can wait. Do you want some water? Want to lie down?"

Her cheeks heated even more. "Stop. Just go, do what you need to do. I'm fine. Or I will be. I just... heck, I don't know what my problem is. But I'll be okay in a few minutes."

Instead of leaving her, he sat beside her and put his ridiculously warm, solid arm around her shoulders. Part of her wanted to push him away for being so nice to her after everything she'd done. The other part wanted to sink against him, maybe even slide her own arm around his waist. Good grief. What was wrong with her tonight?

"I can practically see the wheels spinning in that sharp brain of yours," he teased. "You're not used to feeling vulnerable. But you need to give yourself a break. The stress is getting to you. It would get to anyone in your position. And it's only going to get worse in the next few weeks."

She groaned and sat back, forcing him to move his arm before she embarrassed herself even more and leaned against him.

"As much as I hate to admit it, I think you may be right. It feels as if a giant boulder is crashing down a mountain toward me. I can't seem to get out of the way no matter how fast I run. And yet, I'm not the one in peril. Joey is." She clenched her fists and opened her eyes. "I don't have time to sit here doing nothing while the clock is ticking away the remaining hours of his life."

She started to get up, but he gently pressed her back down.

"You're not going to help your brother like this. You're running on empty. And all that guilt you're carrying around is making you miserable. Those people, the Claremonts, obviously care a great deal about you. And it sounds like you've done a lot more for them over the years besides a few visits here and there. From what I heard, you have nothing to feel guilty about where they're concerned, far from it. And you've done everything you can to help your brother. You're still doing everything you can. Give yourself permission for some downtime now and then. Otherwise you'll run out of gas and won't be able to do anything for him."

She let out a shaky breath. He was right, about running on empty. She barely slept anymore. And her concentration was shot. But he was wrong that she shouldn't feel guilty. She had far more to feel guilty about than he knew.

He needed to know the truth. She needed to tell him what she'd done. But if she did, would he quit trying to help Joey? If she didn't, would someone else be hurt, because of her lie?

Think, Raine. Figure it out. There has to be a way to fix this without sacrificing Joey in the process.

"You seem better. If you're up for it, we can talk it through," he said.

She looked up, startled. Had she spoken out loud? "Talk it through?"

"The attack, what happened here. I've read the police reports, or as much as I could in only one night, plus yesterday at the hospital. You've probably read them dozens, maybe hundreds of times over the years. I heard Joey's bare-bones version of events earlier in the limited time that we had with him. But that's still not enough. Let's talk it out, use each other as a sounding board. Then I'll look around, with that in my head, so I can picture what happened and look for holes in the theories the police formed."

Relief had her eagerly grabbing on to the lifeline that he'd given her. She'd avoid confessing her terrible secret for a little while longer. And maybe before that, just maybe, something would click in Callum's investigator mind, something that would be the answer to her, and Joey's, prayers.

"All right." She drew a deep breath, her shakiness easing. "How do we start?"

"For now, let's limit it to the inside of the house. We can discuss the rest after we leave so we're not keeping the Claremonts away longer than necessary. Although I did want to ask about pets. I'm guessing they don't have any now or they'd have said something."

"They don't. And they didn't back then either, if that's your next question. No dog to bark and alert anyone."

"Neighbors? The homes aren't that close together. But if one of them had a dog who tended to alert when someone came around, that would be good to know. Might be indicative of whether the killer was known in the neighborhood or not."

She shook her head. "I've heard dogs in the neighborhood before, but not close by. I don't think any of the houses right around this one had dogs back then."

"All right. We'll move on then. Talk it through."

"We focus on Alicia?"

"For now. We'll talk potential suspects later. Alicia was twenty, a sophomore at Athens Technical College. She still lived with her parents to save money."

She nodded, sitting forward. "She was pursuing a nursing degree. She wanted to help people." Her stomach knotted. Alicia, from all accounts, had been a good student, a good person. She could have made a difference in the world.

"It was a Friday night, Saturday morning, really. She'd been blowing off steam at a local club. Left around two a.m. and drove home."

Raine nodded. "Her parents were out of town for the weekend, visiting a sick friend. They weren't sure they'd be back early enough Monday for Alicia to make it to her first class. So they all agreed she'd stay here."

Callum stood. "If you're better now, I'll walk it through. You can sit and—"

"No. No, I'm good. Really. I want to help."

He held out his hand.

She hesitated, then let him pull her to her feet. Instead of immediately letting go, he smiled and led her toward the foyer. It wasn't as if they were really holding hands. Not as if they were a couple or anything. But it had been so long since she'd touched another person that his hand on hers seemed like a warm hug that went all through her body. And when they reached the foyer, and he pulled his hand free, she suddenly felt bereft, alone, sad.

He frowned. "You sure you're up to this?"

"Yes, yes, of course. Sorry, was just thinking." She smiled, her face heating once again with embarrassment. "Go on. I've never done a walk-through before, or whatever you called it. I'm not sure how this goes."

"There aren't any rules or procedures. It's just the two of us talking it through, walking the scene to the best of our ability." He stood with his back to the front door and waved her over to do the same.

"We're standing where Alicia would have stood that night," he said. "The crime scene photos focused on the bedroom where the police believe everything happened. You've seen the house before, since a few months after the trial. Is it similar to that night or completely different now?"

She scanned the foyer, the arched openings to the left and right, the family room straight ahead. "Huh. I never thought about it before. But I don't think much has changed ever since I started visiting them. It's kind of...frozen in time. How sad."

"It might give them comfort leaving things much as they were when their daughter was around. When I stand here, as if coming through the front door, I see most of the living room. If the furniture is in the same location—"

"It is."

"—then there really aren't any hiding places in there. If the couch had been on the far wall, facing us, I'd say the perpetrator could have hidden behind it. But we're facing the side of the couch, and the mirror above the fireplace mantel shows the other side of it."

"Oh, wow. I didn't think about that."

"If he was in the family room, she'd have seen him as soon as she walked in the door and could have run outside."

"That makes sense." She motioned to her right. "What about the kitchen?"

"Let's check it out." He stepped through the archway into the small, galley-style kitchen, moving all the way to the end. There was a door that led into the carport area. And another one beside it, at the end of the row of cabinets. "The police report said there were no indications anyone came through this door. But there was no sign of forced entry on the front door either."

"Which is why it makes sense that she must have known her attacker. And Joey had never met Alicia."

He opened the door inside the kitchen. "The pantry. It's not a walk-in. No way for someone to hide inside unless they were a small child and could crawl onto one of the shelves." He closed the door. "As for her knowing Joey, that's in dispute, as we already discussed."

"Randy Hagen lied. And him saying he saw the

two together just goes to show that he knew her on sight even though he told the police he didn't."

"His testimony was that he saw pictures of her on the news and remembered seeing her with Joey."

"As I said, fabrications."

"How do you know he lied? Because that's what Joey said?"

She lifted her chin. "Yes. And because there weren't any corroborating witnesses. No one else at the bar remembered seeing either of them that night."

"That's not what I remember reading. Others said they thought they saw them, but weren't sure."

She crossed her arms.

"Her credit card statement proves she was there," he continued. "The place was loud, crowded, dark. She didn't do anything to stand out. But she was definitely there. Joey could have been too. If he wasn't, why would Hagen lie about it? What did he have to gain?"

"Revenge. He and Joey both liked the same girl a few years earlier. She dumped Hagen for Joey. That's why they weren't friends anymore."

"Years earlier. And Hagen decides to get back at him by helping send him to death row? Seems extreme." He held up his hands to stop anything she might say in response. "Let's leave that discussion for another time. Back to the question of how the killer got inside the home. The police theorized that Joey rummaged through her purse at the bar and found her spare key. Her parents confirmed she always kept a spare in an inside purse pocket, in case the three of them were heading out of town together. She had a friend who lived on campus who'd watch the place, check it out, make sure a pipe hadn't burst or something like that. The spare key wasn't in her purse when the police found it."

"She could have lost it at any time and just not realized it."

"Maybe," he conceded, not sounding convinced.

"I still think she must have let the killer in," Raine said.

"Or they had a key. All we have is speculation and theories on that right now. The windows were locked. None of the screens were ripped. Neither outside door showed scratches or signs of having been jimmied open. The frames were intact."

"Then the police have to be wrong that he was waiting inside. Maybe she came home with someone she knew and he came inside with her."

"You're thinking Hagen?" he asked.

She shrugged. "Possibly."

"Did she know Hagen?"

"No one's ever proved it. But they haven't proved Joey did either." She arched a brow in challenge.

He smiled and turned around in the kitchen, glancing from the stove to the refrigerator, the countertops. "Normally, in a situation like this, I'd say someone could use a ruse like a pizza delivery to get her to open the door. They could pretend they had accidentally gone to the wrong house. They'd take the box with them when they left so no one would know. Or a package delivery. Any number of things to get someone to open the door for a stranger. But at that time of morning, I just don't see it."

"I don't either, honestly. I sure wouldn't open the door after midnight for anyone I didn't know," she agreed.

"Another possibility is that someone was hiding in the shrubs by the front door. When she opened it, he stepped in behind her, forced his way inside."

She slowly nodded. "Sounds plausible. But I don't remember the police saying anything about that in their reports."

"They probably didn't find any dirt or leaves inside to support the theory so they didn't mention it."

"It's a window for reasonable doubt, though. A small one, but more than I had before. Thank you."

He smiled. "She may have simply forgotten to lock the door behind herself too, and someone else came in after she did."

She blinked. "That's so obvious, and yet no one— not even me—has brought that up before either."

"I'm sure the police considered all of that. But the detectives would have gone over everything and put the puzzle together the way they think made the most sense."

"That my brother did it."

"Hagen gave them his name. Then Joey confessed. Hard to fault them for believing he was their guy." He held up his hands again. "Let's not talk about false confessions just yet. We'll deal with that later."

She let out a frustrated breath. "What next then?"

"For now, let's assume no one forced their way inside with her. What did she do when she locked the door behind her? Her purse was found on that decorative table beside the front door. Her keys were on top. The kitchen and family room were neat, clean. Nothing to suggest she went into the kitchen for a snack. No pillows out of place or a blanket or throw wrinkled on the back of the couch to suggest she watched TV after coming in."

Raine stood with her back to the door again, an eerie feeling settling over her as she imagined herself in Alicia's position. Coming into the warm, cozy home she'd grown up in, not knowing that her young life was about to come to a horrific end. She went through the motions of putting a purse and keys on the little table, even though her purse was locked in Callum's SUV. Then she looked down. "Shoes. I would have taken off my shoes at my house and put them in the hall closet."

He joined her in the foyer. "There isn't a closet in this little entryway. Bedroom maybe?"

"Maybe." She moved around the corner into the hallway. The first door on the left was more narrow than the others. She pulled it open. Sure enough, it was a closet. Coats and sweaters hung neatly on a pole. And a wooden rack sat beneath them on the floor with several pairs of shoes in it. When she closed the door, it squeaked. "The killer would have heard that."

"If it squeaked back then, and if he was already inside. But I think he would have already known she was inside. He'd hear the front door, or her keys and purse being left on the table. The police theory is that he was waiting in her bedroom. It faces the front yard. They reasoned the perpetrator peeked through the blinds, watching for her arrival."

"All supposition. Guesses. They didn't find any fingerprints to prove it."

He smiled. "That's why they said her murder was premeditated. The killer wore gloves."

"More guesses."

"Educated guesses. It's unlikely that someone could have attacked her and strangled her without leaving DNA or fingerprints unless they wore gloves. And a condom. There was evidence of rape but no semen."

She shivered. "Poor Alicia."

His jaw tightened. "Poor Alicia." He led the way down the hall, looking briefly inside each room they came upon, as if he was creating a map in his mind. In the main bedroom, he studied the pictures on the walls, used his phone camera to capture the images, as well as some of the collections arranged on the top of the dresser.

"You think the killer came into this room too?" Raine asked from the doorway.

"I think if he did, then knowledge of anything in these various rooms is something he'd have, a way to prove his identity if he mentions anything here. There weren't any pictures of these rooms in the police reports, nothing in the press releases. And I remember the responding officer said all of the doors in this hall were closed, except the last one."

"Alicia's room."

He nodded and stepped into the parents' walk-in closet. The back boasted white wallpaper with sprays of purple flowers across it. Again, he took a picture, likely because that was a detail he hadn't known before. Then the two of them headed into the hall. They paused just outside of the door to the room that they'd specifically come here tonight to see.

Alicia's room. The place where she'd been attacked, beaten, sexually assaulted, and then strangled and left for her parents to discover Monday morning when they'd returned from out of town.

She'd suffered a brutal death. Whoever had killed her deserved the worst punishment the courts could offer. And her parents deserved justice, the knowledge that whoever had killed their daughter had paid for their crime. Raine wanted that for them just as badly as they did. But not at the cost of Joey's life. Joey was kind, sweet, or had been as a child, even as a teenager. He'd been bullied, not the kind who'd bullied others. Yes, he'd gotten into trouble, robbing homes, graffiti, property crimes. And he'd done some minor jail time for it. But none of his crimes had ever been against people. He'd never been violent. And he'd pleaded guilty each time he was caught.

Callum put his hand on the knob. "Ready?"

She drew a bracing breath. "Ready."

He pushed the door open.

Raine pressed a hand to her chest. "Oh, dear sweet Lord."

Chapter Eleven

"Not what you expected to see?" Callum asked, not sure why Raine was so shocked.

She slowly shook her head. "It looks...it looks as if Alicia could come home any minute. I thought you'd get an idea of the size of the room, where the closet was, the window, that sort of thing. I had no idea they'd kept it the way it was all those years ago." Her gaze flew to the bed. "Except...that's different. Similar, but not exactly the same as the bedding in the photos."

"The police would have taken the original bedding as evidence. Her parents probably tried to find new bedding like it, but it was discontinued or they couldn't locate the same set. Judging by how everything else looks, her books, her computer—no doubt returned after your brother's case was adjudicated— high school trophies, posters on the wall, they tried to keep it the same. A memorial to their daughter."

"They definitely haven't moved on."

"Many families don't. Alicia may have technically been an adult. But her parents thought of her as their child, their only child. Getting rid of her things must have proved too painful in the beginning. Later, they just closed the door and left it alone. Although, I'd say from the lack of dust in here, it's being cleaned regularly."

"How sad to imagine them doing that." She ran her hands up and down her arms as if chilled. "What did you want to see in here?"

He pulled out his phone and thumbed across the screen, then held it up. "This album contains all of the police photographs taken in the room. Originally, as you said, I wanted to get the feel of the space, the dimensions. But since the original crime scene is so well-preserved, we have a unique opportunity to compare it to the police pictures. If there are any significant details in here not photographed, again, that provides us with information only the true killer would know about."

"Which would help you prove someone else did it if we come up with a suspect."

"It could." Or it could pile on additional proof against Joey Quintero if Callum got another chance to interview him—without Raine present. He'd contact his prison-admin friend tonight and work on getting that set up.

"All right," Raine said, seemingly encouraged. "Let's see what you have there."

He handed her the phone, not feeling that he needed to look at the pictures right now since he'd studied them in-depth last night. Instead, he walked the length and breadth of the room. The closet was small, like everything else in the home. White wooden bifold doors opened accordion style. Not a walk-in, but someone could easily hide inside, behind the hanging clothes, and peer through the slats in the doors. It was typical of many homes built in the same era.

When he swept aside some of the pink hangers, it revealed that the back of the closet was covered with wallpaper. It was white with repeating patterns of pink sprays of flowers clinging to tree branches. His guess was that they were cherry blossoms, but he wasn't sure. He'd have to take a picture before they left since he hadn't seen this in any photos of this room.

To the right of the closet was the wall facing the street, and opposite the full-size bed. Like the wooden bed, the chest of drawers and small desk on the window wall were white. When he pushed down on one of the aluminum blinds to check the window lock, he saw the frame was nailed shut. He'd have to ask the Claremonts about that since he didn't know if that was the way it had been fifteen years ago or a more recent change. Given the current state of everything else in the room, likely it was done way back then and just wasn't noted in a police report.

Which was disappointing and encouraging at the same time.

Disappointing, because he'd expect more of his fellow detectives. Encouraging in that it meant not everything was documented, so he and Raine had a chance of finding something that might steer them in a new direction.

Or confirm Joey's guilt.

"Do you think any of these books in her desk drawers are relevant?" Raine asked.

He glanced over to see what she'd found, a stash of books in the bottom drawer, seven or eight from the looks of it. More books sat on sagging shelves attached to the wall opposite the closet. Apparently, Alicia was a prolific reader. There was a broad range of nonfiction and fiction books in many genres.

"Couldn't hurt. You never know what the killer may have done in here before or after killing Alicia. He may remember some of those books, for whatever reason. If he does, that's great evidence to prove he was in this room. They aren't in plain sight, not in the police photos. Good job, Raine."

She smiled and began snapping pictures of them.

Callum was relieved to see her smile again. She'd seemed so lost earlier, as if the weight of the world—and her brother's alleged crime—was on her shoulders and hers alone. While Callum doubted those books in the drawer would help them, it made her feel as if she was furthering the investigation. And one never knew for sure what small detail might bring an entire puzzle into focus.

They spent a good deal of time in the room, noting every detail. But aside from getting a feel for the layout, and lack of hiding places, about all Callum felt they had as additional potentially significant information to note were the pink hangers in the closet, the wallpaper and those books Raine had found in the desk.

He was just about to suggest they leave the room when he looked in the last place he'd almost forgotten to look. Up. They were faint, hard to see with the light on. But they were there. He crossed to the light switch and flipped it off.

Raine gasped beside him as she too looked up. "Glow-in-the-dark stars. They're all over the ceiling."

Callum snapped a picture. "Definitely not something the average person looking at police photos would know about. But the killer, if he was in this room with the light out, would definitely have noticed them." He flipped the light back on and the stars almost completely disappeared, fading in with the textured ceiling.

"I had those when I was a teenager," Raine said, her voice sad. "It's sweet that she kept them even as a young adult going to college. They were probably sentimental to her."

"I had them too. But mine had planets and spaceships."

She smiled again, but this time it was much more subdued. "Can we get out of here now?"

"After you."

They returned to the foyer.

"Do you want to look in the new part of the home too?" Raine motioned toward the door in the back left side of the family room.

Callum hesitated. "Since it wasn't here during the crime, it's probably not necessary. But now that you've mentioned it, let's take a quick look just in case it makes us think of something else that we need to ask the Claremonts."

He pushed open the door and they stepped into a large room with a soaring ceiling. Where the rest of the house was stuck in time, this addition was the epitome of modern, black-and-white industrial design. A huge TV hung on the far wall. Comfortable-looking white leather couches formed a U-shape facing the TV. To the left and right of the TV were expansive sliding glass doors with black iron grids that led out onto a stone deck with an outdoor kitchen tucked into one side.

"Wow," Raine said. "This is super nice. I'll bet this is where they spend most of their time. I sure would."

He looked up at the black beams on the soaring ceiling. "From the outside you'd think it was two stories. But it's really only one, with high ceilings."

"I'm glad they have this. It's nice to know they don't spend all of their time in the past. This is a happy room." She turned around and the smile died on her face. "Oh no."

Callum turned to see what she'd seen. His heart sank when he saw what could only be described as a shrine to the Claremonts' dead daughter. Row upon row of pictures filled the massive wall, showing Alicia in various phases of her life, from birth, to toddler, to teen and finally a few, though not many, from her college years. It appeared that every picture had been carefully chosen to only show happy times because in every single one, Alicia was smiling at the camera.

Raine rubbed her arms again. "I've never, not my entire adult life, ever doubted my brother. I've never thought he did this. But I've also never realized the full extent of how Alicia's death hurt the Claremonts, until now." She turned to face him. "I don't want this to happen to another family if there's some way for me to prevent it. We need to leave. Right now."

She hurried toward the door.

He raced after her but didn't catch up until she was in the foyer about to open the front door.

"Wait, Raine. Just wait." He grabbed her shoulder and gently turned her around. "What's wrong? I mean besides the obvious, that you're sad about Alicia's family. And worried about Joey."

She shook her head, her hair flying around her shoulders. "It's far worse than any of that." Tears spilled down her cheeks. "We have to go. I need to talk to you, to tell you... I lied, Callum. I kept a terrible secret. I didn't think it would matter, but then you said... And then I saw... I can't—"

"Breathe, Raine. Just breathe. Whatever it is, it can't be that bad."

Her eyes squeezed shut, tears dripping down her cheeks. "I did something awful. And if I don't fix it, if I don't tell you what I did, another woman might die."

Chapter Twelve

After seeing physical proof of the pain the Claremonts had suffered all these years, were still suffering, it was one of the hardest things Raine had ever done to speak to Mrs. Claremont on the phone without breaking down. But Callum had insisted they leave the house and that she tell the Claremonts they could return before she made her confession.

Confession was supposed to be good for the soul. But Raine feared it was going to destroy her. Still, *not* confessing would be even worse, because someone else could be hurt.

She ended the call and slid her phone into her purse on the console between them. "Done," she said. "They finished dinner in town and were driving around the area waiting for my call. They're heading home right now. She was so sweet, so worried about me, about us." She shook her head. "I don't understand how she does it. And I certainly don't deserve it." She clutched her hands together in her lap. "Can we pull over now, so we can talk?"

"Just a few more minutes. I don't want to be sitting on the side of the road and the Claremonts pass by and stop to check on us."

"Oh, gosh, no. Good thinking." She finally focused on their surroundings. "You're going into town. My house isn't far from here. We could go there. Eat later, assuming you still want to be around me."

"I'm sure whatever you want to tell me isn't nearly as bad as you think. And, yes, I was already planning on going to your place first."

"You know my address? Wait, of course you do. You looked me up online, accused me of living in a mansion."

"What's good for the goose—"

"Is good for the gander. I know, I know. I followed you, searched for your information online. It's only fair that you do the same. I get it. Doesn't mean I like it, but I get it."

He turned down the lane that led to only one place, the gated community where she lived.

"Do you have a key fob or something so we can get through the guard gate?"

She smiled, vaguely amused in spite of the stress that was ready to tear her apart. "We won't need a key fob, or a sticker on the windshield, anything like that. Just slow down and use the owner lane when we're at the guard shack. And roll your window down."

He gave her a puzzled look but nodded.

When they arrived at the gate, he stayed to the right, avoiding the few cars lined up in the visitor lane speaking to the guard.

"Excuse me for a sec." She unbuckled her seat

belt and leaned over him toward his window. A few seconds later, a beep sounded and the gate began to swing open.

"Well, I'll be damned." Callum glanced at her. "Some kind of facial recognition, right? There was a camera hidden somewhere?"

"In the bushes, so we don't have to look at an ugly pole with a camera on top as we smile and go on through."

"Rich people." He shook his head. "Eccentric and strange. But kind of cool."

"Rich people? If I'm wealthy, what are you? Your salary at UB—"

"Is none of your business."

"And readily available, at least the range, if you search hard enough. Calling me rich like it's a bad thing is pretty lame when you earn close to what I do, maybe more. And neither of us needs to apologize for what we have. We both rose from modest backgrounds and worked our butts off to create opportunities. No one ever handed me anything I didn't earn, that's for darn sure."

He smiled as he made a right turn onto her street. "My apologies for apparently being a snob and not realizing it."

She clasped her hands together again. "You're not the one who owes anyone an apology. And you're never going to forgive me once I tell you what I did. I just pray you'll please, please think about it before you react. My brother shouldn't die because of my mistakes. I need your help, desperately, to help him."

"You honestly think whatever this thing is that you've done, this secret, is going to make me quit the investigation?"

She winced. "If I was in your position, yes. But I'm banking on you being a better person than me."

He chuckled and motioned toward the windshield as he pulled into the circular brick driveway at the front of her house. "Honey, we're home."

Raine led the way up the front walk with a mixture of dread and anticipation. She dreaded their upcoming conversation. But she was looking forward to being home. It had been weeks since she'd last been here and she was tired of living out of a suitcase. Having a hot shower in her own bathroom would be a treat. And getting to sleep in her own bed, heaven.

But first, a little hell. She had to face the consequences of what she'd done.

At the door, he stopped beside her. "Let me guess, facial recognition again?"

"Actually, no. I've never been that great with electronics. And the idea of being locked out of my home because of a power outage or computer issue scares me. I prefer the old-fashioned method." She pulled a key out of her purse.

He grinned. "Good to know that I'm not the only one."

"Who uses a key?"

"Who has trouble with electronics. Don't tell Asher that I admitted it. He teases me enough as it is."

She smiled and pushed open the door, then sucked in a shocked breath at the devastation inside.

Callum swore and pushed her behind him, a gun suddenly in his hand. "Get in the car and lock the doors. Call 911. Do it. Now."

She took off running toward his SUV.

Chapter Thirteen

Callum stepped around an overturned table in the massive, two-story foyer, sweeping his pistol left and right. Gray-and-white marbled floors were probably the fashion star of the entire home. But they were currently littered with broken dishes and glasses, shredded pillows, and decorative tables and chairs either knocked over or splintered into kindling. Whoever had trashed her house wasn't in it for robbery. Or if they were, it was an afterthought. They'd come prepared to do damage. What he needed to find out was whether they were still here, and whether they were armed.

In spite of the cavernous feel of the entryway and main room beyond it, which also sported a two-story ceiling, the first floor didn't boast many rooms, at least, not separate ones. Open concept, he thought he'd heard it called. He could see foyer to main room to the backyard, and kitchen and dining areas by standing in one spot and turning around. No one was there. Which meant they were either in the back hall underneath the curved, sweeping staircase, on the second floor or long gone.

He was hoping they were still here. Because he really wanted to wring their neck. Raine didn't need this kind of stress or fear lumped on top of everything else she was going through right now.

Trying to avoid crunching any of the glass beneath his shoes, he quietly made his way under the stairs. A handful of doors opened off the little hall back there. One by one, he threw them open and aimed his pistol inside. Empty, all of them. These rooms— an office, two guest bedrooms and a bathroom—had been spared the vandalism done to the other areas.

A thump sounded overhead.

Callum smiled. The jerk was still here. He eased back to the foyer, then rushed around the bottom of the stairs, aiming his gun toward the landing at the top. Clear. No one there, or at least, not where he could see them.

Ever so slowly and carefully, he crept up the shiny marble stairs toward the second floor. As soon as he reached the top, another thump sounded, off to his right. There were a ridiculous number of doors off the wide landing. And a skylight overhead allowed the waning sunlight to keep the shadows at bay. Aside from a couple of overstuffed chairs and one low side table, there weren't any hiding places on the landing. The perp had to be in one of the rooms, if they even realized Callum was here.

There were three doors to check close to where he'd heard the last sound. He stood frozen in place, barely breathing as he tried not to make any noise that would alert his prey. When another minute ticked by without anything, he figured the game was up. The person he was after must have realized someone was here and was trying to be quiet now too.

He aimed the pistol in his right hand up toward the ceiling while he grabbed the doorknob for the first door. He quickly swung it open, ducking down as he rushed inside, sweeping his pistol around. A bedroom. He cleared the attached bathroom and closet, then peered out the opening. Clear.

The second door led to another bedroom, also empty. He was just about to open the third door on this side of the landing when he heard the crunching of glass downstairs. He swore. The perp must have gotten past him when he was checking the other two rooms. He whirled around and ran to the top of the stairs and aimed his pistol down them.

Nothing.

Slowly, carefully, he descended the stairs, looking all around. When he reached the bottom, he glanced toward the back wall of the house, which was mostly floor-to-ceiling windows with three sets of double French doors. All were closed. Looking toward the foyer, he saw the front door was closed too. Which meant the bad guy was either in one of the rooms under the stairs now, or outside.

Raine is outside.

Ah, hell.

He took off running toward the front door and threw it open.

A pistol was aimed directly at his chest. It was

Raine, pointing her gun at him. He swore and grabbed it, yanking it away from her.

"I'm sorry, I'm sorry," she said. "I thought you were the bad guy."

"And I thought he was outside and you were in danger. Why aren't you in the car, doors locked, like I told you?"

"I was, but you were gone too long. I got worried and—behind you!"

He whirled around.

A figure dressed all in black took off through the family room toward the back doors.

"Halt, or I'll shoot," Callum yelled, sprinting after him.

The perp flipped a dead bolt and flung open a French door.

"Lock yourself in one of the rooms downstairs," Callum yelled back to Raine. Then he ran out the open door toward the fleeing figure.

Ten minutes later, Callum swore a blue streak and headed toward Raine's home. The back of her property faced a wooded area that appeared to be some kind of huge nature preserve. He'd done his best to follow the fleeing man but he'd lost him. If Raine wasn't waiting at her house, he'd have kept searching. But he didn't trust her not to come looking for him again. And he didn't want her in these woods with a potentially armed criminal hiding out here.

By the time he reached the house, the police were there, crawling all over the place. He had to drop his pistol and explain who he was to two uniformed cops.

Raine stepped out and told them he wasn't the bad guy, that he was the detective she'd told them about.

"Private investigator," Callum corrected. "Formerly a detective with the Athens-Clarke County Police Department."

"Give him back his weapon. He's one of the good guys," a man in a gray business suit said as he joined Raine on the patio. "It's been a hot minute, Callum. Good to see you again."

"Danny, hey. What's it been, a couple of months?" Callum took his pistol from one of the officers and slid it into the inside pocket of his jacket. "I chased the intruder into the woods but he disappeared. I never saw a weapon, but he could very well be armed."

Danny issued instructions and several police went off in pursuit.

"Let's get back inside." Callum steered Raine toward the open French doors. "If the intruder does have a gun, I don't want to give him a target."

The three of them headed to a grouping of white leather chairs and a couch in front of an equally white fireplace. This furniture had been spared being slashed with a knife, probably because Callum and Raine had interrupted his little vandalism party.

"You two are friends?" Raine glanced back and forth between them.

The detective laughed. "I guess you could say that. I married his sister. And we were partners in homicide for three years."

"More like partners in crime," Callum teased.

Raine frowned. "I don't understand."

Danny waved toward Callum. "In spite of being one of the best detectives we've ever had, Callum decided to take an undercover gig for almost a year to help bring down a crime ring in Athens. He dragged me into it and we were badass fake criminals. Pardon my language, ma'am."

She smiled. "No worries. I've heard far worse, probably said it too."

He laughed, then sobered and motioned toward the destruction around them. "It's a shame someone broke in and did all this damage. Looks like a nice place. I know you told me you didn't get a good look at the perpetrator. What about you, Callum? Can you give me a description? I'll put out a BOLO."

"BOLO?" Raine asked.

"Be on the lookout," Callum explained. "Old cop shows used to say APB, all-points bulletin. Same thing. Just tells law enforcement to keep an eye out for someone. Five-eight, slim build, maybe a hundred seventy pounds. Dressed all in black, including his shoes, gloves and knit hat pulled down low around his neck and over his ears. I only managed a glimpse of his profile, not a straight-on look at him. He's white, dark brown hair sticking out of the bottom of his hat, could be anywhere from midtwenties to late thirties. It's not much, I know."

Raine blinked. "It's a lot more than I got. All I could tell Detective Cooper was that he was dressed like a ninja."

Danny chuckled. "Told you Callum was one of the best. Still is, I imagine. Working for that cold case company now. Ms. Quintero said you're helping with her brother's case."

"Looking into it, yes. Turns out, it's one I gophered on years ago, for Farley."

The detective winced. "I didn't wish the guy dead, but can't say I miss working with him."

"Raine believes he pressured her brother into a false confession."

Danny's brows raised in surprise. "Well, now. He was unorthodox, tough. But I've never heard anyone accuse him of that before. Got any proof?"

Callum intervened. "I've been in touch with a professor in the criminal justice studies program at the University of Georgia, in Athens. She's studying the interview report on Joey so she can offer an opinion on whether it could have been a false confession." Raine looked at him in surprise and he realized he'd never gotten around to telling her about the professor. "She's an expert in the field. When our liaison called for the files on the case, she wasn't able to get any recordings of Mr. Quintero's interviews, said Farley apparently never recorded them. You worked with him more than I did, and more recently. Was that unusual for him?"

"Good question. I know he griped about modern technology because he wasn't good with it." His mouth quirked. "Kind of like someone else I know."

"Whatever. Does that mean he avoided it?"

Danny nodded. "When he could get away with it. Honestly, it wouldn't surprise me if a lot of his interviews were done the old-fashioned way, pen and paper, no audio or video. It doesn't mean anything improper was going on. But I can look into it, let you know what I find, see if there was any kind of suspicious pattern to his interrogations."

"I'd appreciate it. We're in a hurry too."

Danny glanced at Raine, a sympathetic look on his face. "Understood. I'll get back to you as soon as I can. I'll focus on trying to find a pattern in the cases around the same time period as Mr. Quintero's. But I have to work this scene first and file my report."

He picked up a computer tablet he must have left on a side table earlier. "Ms. Quintero gave me her version of what happened while you were chasing the suspect. Let's hear it from your point of view, Callum."

Danny was just as thorough as Callum remembered him being when they'd worked together. While Raine was sent to inventory the home and determine if anything was actually taken, instead of just destroyed, Danny grilled Callum on every detail of Callum's search of the home. By the time he started in on the details of his chase through the woods, Raine had already reported back that nothing was taken and was sitting on the couch with him again.

Danny shifted in his chair across from them. "All right. Let's see if there's anything else I need to add, another wrinkle that might tell me whether this is some nut or a drunk college frat boy out vandalizing homes, or something more."

Raine's eyes widened. "What do you mean, something more?"

"It seems awfully coincidental that you two are in town working on a murder case and your house gets broken into. Maybe the bad guy came here looking for your notes to see what you might have found out, and got mad and tore the place up when he didn't find any."

She went pale and twisted her hands in her lap. "Then it's a good thing my computer isn't here. Or my printed-out files."

"Hold on," Callum said. "Going down that path assumes someone would have a reason to worry about the investigation. It was resolved in the courts and we've yet to find evidence of anyone else being involved in Ms. Claremont's murder."

Raine's eyes flashed with anger. "I told you, Joey's innocent. It makes perfect sense that the real murderer would be worried about me digging into his case."

Danny held up his hands. "Hang on. You two want to argue, do it on your time. I'm just getting the background here so I cover every possibility. Callum, you mentioned earlier that you and Ms. Quintero had just come back from speaking to the Claremonts about what happened when their daughter was killed."

"More like I wanted firsthand knowledge of the crime scene's layout, the neighborhood and geography around it. I wasn't going to bother the parents of the deceased unless or until I felt it was absolutely necessary. However, since Raine has a close friendship with the deceased's parents, we took advantage of that and were able to tour their home. A few hours later, we came back here to review the case and make our plans for what to do tomorrow."

"And once you arrived, you opened the door and found that the home had been ransacked."

"Exactly."

"But nothing was stolen. Seems odd that someone would have done so much damage without stealing anything." He motioned to the broken side table, papers scattered on the floor, the shredded pillows strewed around. "There's emotion here, anger. And it seems to be directed at you, Ms. Quintero. You told me earlier that you don't know anyone who'd want to hurt you. Regardless of whether or not your brother is guilty, is there anything you've done, perhaps before Callum was involved in the case, that could have made someone feel threatened, or angry? Something related to the case you're working?"

She stared at him, her brow furrowed. "I honestly don't know. It's not like we've spoken to anyone today except my brother at the prison, and the Claremonts. No one else knew we were coming to town today. My brother's lawyers have been interviewing people off and on in town recently. And I was asking questions around town too, but that was weeks ago. I suppose Randy Hagen could have heard about all that and wanted to punish me by breaking in and tearing things up. He lied under oath in the trial against my brother. For all I know, he may be the one who killed Alicia Claremont."

Callum exchanged a pained look with Danny. "You can look into him if you want. But he had an alibi during the time when Alicia was attacked. I can't see him having a motive to vandalize Raine's property."

"Maybe you should look into his alibi," Raine insisted.

Danny glanced back and forth between them, looking puzzled. "Alibi for the break-in or the murder fifteen years ago?"

"Break-in," Callum said.

"Murder," Raine said, at the same time. She glanced at Callum, her aggravation dissolving into a look of guilt. "There are other cases I've been looking into. Perhaps this is related to those. We came here tonight so I could tell Callum that—"

Callum stood, interrupting her. "We're wasting Danny's time. He doesn't need all the details about the other cases UB is investigating."

Danny stood, looking relieved. "I'll put out a BOLO specifically for Hagen as well as one on our unknown intruder. They could be one and the same, but if not, we're covered. I'll send a press release to the media too, get an alert out on the news. If Hagen is around, someone should see him and turn him in. And if he's the intruder, we'll kill two birds with one stone. Callum, if something comes up in this other investigation you're working and you think it could shed light on another suspect—"

"I'll absolutely reach out."

"Good enough for me. It's getting late and I have a report to type up."

Raine looked ready to burst with things she wanted

to tell the detective. Callum put his arm around her shoulders, pulling her close. Danny's brows raised, no doubt thinking something was going on between them. Callum didn't care. It did the trick. It flustered Raine and made her go silent. She was staring up at him in surprise, no doubt trying to figure out how she'd given him the wrong signal somewhere along the way.

Danny looked around, as if searching for the crime scene tech.

"He's gone," Callum told him. "Took some latent prints from the French doors and the stairs while we were talking and left."

Raine finally looked at Danny again, a new mystery gathering her attention. "Why did he look for fingerprints? Callum said the guy was wearing gloves."

"Standard procedure," Danny explained. "Sometimes a criminal won't put gloves on outside a place. They don't want someone seeing the gloves and becoming suspicious enough to call the police. Once inside, they put gloves on and plan on wiping down the front door on their way out. But Callum sent our guy fleeing, so he might not have had a chance to wipe any prints away. We may luck out and get an ID."

He glanced around, as if looking for the other policemen and women. But he was the only one there now.

"Son of a… They all left me. Again."

Callum laughed. "You always were one of the last at any scene."

Danny grinned. "Guess not much has changed since we worked together. Callum, once your current investigation is wrapped up, maybe you can stop by the house for dinner. I enjoy watching the games with you at your place. But it'd be nice to host you at our house every once in a while. It would be great to have you and Lucy together again. She misses you."

Callum kept smiling, but it wasn't easy. "Lucy doesn't miss me, Danny. Neither does anyone else in my family. They haven't for many, many years. But I appreciate you lying just the same. Don't forget to look into Farley's records when you can."

Danny shook his head, but didn't argue or deny the truth. "Will do. Ms. Quintero, I'm sorry about what happened to your beautiful home. Athens PD will do everything we can to catch the bad guy. And for tonight, at least, my boss has approved having a couple of patrol cars canvassing the neighborhood, for added security."

"Thank you. I appreciate it."

Danny gave Callum a two-fingered salute and headed toward the foyer.

As soon as the door closed behind Danny, Raine threw Callum's arm off her shoulder and turned to face him. "Explain to me why you kept interrupting me when I was trying to tell Detective Cooper about my work on the serial killer investigation, information that could be related to the break-in."

"It's not."

"How would you know?"

"I'll explain, after you explain something to me.

Where the hell did you get another gun? And where did you hide it so the police wouldn't find it, since my brother-in-law failed to mention anything about it?"

Chapter Fourteen

Raine poked him in the chest. Callum could tell she wasn't the least bit intimidated. Damn she was sexy when she was angry.

She poked him again to emphasize her words as she spoke. "When were you going to tell me you had a false-confession expert lined up for us to talk to? We're supposed to be partners on this case. I'm the one who hired you, not the other way around."

"Is that what you call it when you kidnap someone? Hiring them?"

"Why throw that in my face again? I thought we were way past that."

He shrugged. "Maybe I enjoy riling you up. Stop trying to distract me. Where'd you get the gun? And where is it now?"

"And here I thought you were an investigator."

"It was Faith, wasn't it? She gave it back to you."

Her eyes widened and her face turned a light pink.

He couldn't help but grin. "I love that you blush so easily. You look good with some color in your cheeks.

And it's a dead giveaway, a tell. I always know when you're covering something up."

"So you think," she grumbled.

"What? I'm not sure I heard that."

She cleared her throat. "Don't blame Faith for giving me back my gun. I bought it for protection and wanted it with me in case we have to go into sketchy areas while investigating."

"Don't worry. I won't lambast her for it. She'd just give me a lecture about women's rights until I begged for mercy and forgot why I was mad in the first place."

"I'm liking Faith more and more. As to where I put the gun, I'm not telling. You'll only take it away again."

"Damn straight. I don't want to wake up with it in my face."

"I would never. I mean, not now anyway."

He rolled his eyes. "Good to know."

"You're impossible," she complained. "You never think I can take care of myself. I'll bet the real reason you didn't catch the jerk who broke in is because you were worried about me being here all by my lonesome, unprotected."

"Why would you think that?"

"Look at you. You're in excellent shape. I can't imagine some punk getting away if you were running after him."

"You think I'm in excellent shape, huh?"

"Yeah, well. Don't let it go to your head. It was just a...biological observation. Nothing personal."

He laughed. "Can't say I've heard that one before. I'm going to take it as a compliment." He winked.

She blinked, obviously not sure what to make of that wink. It was so easy to fluster her. He'd probably start doing it more often, just for fun.

She let out a slow deep breath, as if praying for patience. Then she looked up at him, her hands twisting together.

Uh-oh.

"Callum?"

"Raine?"

She sighed. "I told you, when we left the Claremonts, that I had a secret to confess. With everything that happened tonight, I never got the chance. But I can't live with myself if I let one more day go by without telling you the truth."

"Because another woman could die? I think that's what you said earlier."

"Yes. Exactly. And don't take that tone with me."

"What tone?"

"Like you're not taking me seriously. This is important."

"Then I suppose I'd better sit down." He reclined back on the couch. "Nice sofa by the way. This leather is crazy soft."

"Be serious."

"I'm always serious about leather."

She plopped down beside him. "I mean it."

"So do I. Leather is—"

She grabbed his left hand in both of hers. "Pay attention."

The feel of her soft hands holding his had his entire body paying attention. But not in the way she was thinking. As she rattled on about research and files and saving her brother, he pondered when he'd crossed the line from being downright irritated with her and wanting her gone, to being enthralled by the way her hands felt, and how silky her hair looked, and how soft and curvy she was.

Damn. And she was a lawyer to boot.

"Are you listening to me, Callum? Did you hear what I said? Pete Scoggin isn't the serial killer. He's got a criminal record, yes. A friend of mine at the courthouse helped me look up old cases similar to my brother's and his name came up as a suspect in one of them. I included that with the other cases I found and purposely skewed everything to make it look like he could be the real killer. Don't you see? I was desperate, trying to create some kind of carrot to dangle in front of you to convince you to help my brother. I was hoping you'd look into that angle later, after helping me. And by then I could tell you the truth so you didn't waste any time on Scoggin. But you said your team was switching gears, looking at the information I gave you instead of what they were researching before I came along. And that's been scaring me. I'm terrified that looking into the wrong information will allow the real killer time to select another victim. I tried to tell that to Detective Cooper but you stopped me."

Her gaze searched his and she squeezed his hand. "Callum? Why are you looking at me like that?"

"Like what?"

"Like you're…amused. Or something. You should be angry."

"Why would I be angry with you?"

She pulled her hands back and fisted them beside her. "Did you hear anything I just said?"

"Maybe not everything. But I heard most of it."

She stared at him, as if waiting. When he didn't react, she smacked the seat cushion beside her leg. "If that's true, you should be horrified."

He smiled.

Her eyes narrowed. "Why aren't you horrified, Callum? You don't even seem surprised."

"I'm not. You're a lawyer."

She blinked. "And?"

"You're a lawyer who held me at gunpoint and handcuffed me to a chair, not in a good way either."

Her eyes widened.

He decided to take mercy on her. "Look, I wasn't going to take anything you gave me at face value. Asher thought your files seemed golden, that they'd really help. And I'll admit I was hoping they would. But we couldn't risk our entire investigation on your veracity, not until we could prove, or disprove, the information you provided."

"I don't… I don't understand. You told me everyone was focusing on the files that I turned over. I thought you had stopped your original investigation and were relying entirely on my data. That's why I was worried the killer would hurt someone else because you diverted resources."

"We didn't divert resources. I spoke to my boss

and he agreed to add additional investigators to the case so we could look into the new info while continuing with our existing info at the same time."

"You mean, so what happened is, I didn't put anyone in danger by sending you off on a wild-goose chase?"

"Nope."

"You lied."

He arched a brow. "So did you."

She pressed a hand to her brow as if she had a headache. "When, exactly, did you discover my secret, that my information was bogus?"

"It wasn't entirely bogus. You did a lot of good research. You just…extrapolated and exaggerated some of it. As to *when* I realized that? It was the first day, when you were in the hospital. I sat in your room in the ER and did some cross-checking on those new murders you told us about. Asher did the same. We have access to a lot of databases that you don't. It wasn't hard to figure out."

"Are you…are you saying you've been leading me along all this time? I've been dying inside, worried about what I'd done." She stared at him, her green eyes flashing with anger.

"Don't go all sanctimonious on me now. You lied to get what you wanted and I lied because I don't trust lawyers, or criminals, of which you were both. I didn't trust you, don't trust you. And all you've done is proven that I'm right not to do so."

The hurt look in her eyes before she glanced away had him feeling like a heel. He'd answered her questions, but he should have been more delicate in how he'd phrased those answers. Hurting her was never his plan.

"Look, Raine. I didn't mean to—"

"I'll deal with the mess down here later. I'm going upstairs to get a shower. There's a guest room under the stairs that the intruder didn't trash. There are extra linens in the closet, fresh pillows. The kitchen should be well stocked too, except the milk is likely bad now. But the freezer's full. There's also beer, wine, bottled water—"

"Raine. Look at me."

She briefly squeezed her eyes shut, then looked up at him. "Yes?"

"When I said all of that, I was—" His phone buzzed in his pocket. He frowned and pressed the button to silence it without looking at it. "I was answering your questions. But when I did, I should have—" His phone buzzed again. He swore and pulled it out of his pocket to check the screen. It was a text from Asher, with only three characters. 911. He swore again. "I'm sorry, Raine. I have to take this."

"Of course you do. After all, I'm just a lawyer. I'm not even worth your time." She headed toward the stairs.

"Raine, wait."

She jogged up the stairs and disappeared. A moment later, a door slammed overhead.

He started after her, but his phone buzzed again. He stopped and pressed the button to take the call.

"Asher, this had better be a real emergency and not one of your pranks."

"Where are you right now?"

Callum stiffened, his friend's tone telling him this wasn't a joke. "At Raine's house. In Athens. Why?"

"She's there with you?"

"Yes. Her house was broken into. The police just left and she's gone upstairs to take a shower."

"Broken into? Did they catch the guy? I'm assuming you're both okay or you'd have said something."

"We're fine. They haven't caught the guy. Not yet. What's going on? What's the emergency?"

"Remember the name Raine gave us, the guy she said could be the serial killer?"

"Pete Scoggin. But we already determined he had alibis for the killings."

"Most. Not all. There was one we couldn't alibi him out of, so Faith and I did our due diligence just to feel confident that we could mark him off our suspect list. She couldn't prove that he was in that one victim's vicinity during the time of the attack. But she couldn't disprove it either. We've found several links between him and the victim that Raine didn't come close to finding. They were neighbors once, like Raine said. But she didn't know about all of the complaints we found in city hall that the victim made against him. She reported alleged code violations on his property, called animal control because he'd leave his dog chained up without food and water in the backyard, things like that. There were calls to the police too. Noise complaints, vandalism she believed he'd done to her place, that sort of thing."

"Vandalism?" A chill went up his spine as he glanced up the stairs. He headed to the front door to make sure it was locked. Then he checked the back doors too.

"There was other stuff, problems between him, the victim, and other people too," Asher continued. "Sounds like he was that nightmare neighbor who bullied everyone on the street. But the victim was the only one who ever really stood up to him."

"Did the police list him as a suspect in her murder? Sounds like they at least should have interviewed him."

"Nope. The victim moved months before her death. Supposedly it was for a job opportunity. That's what she told her friends. But Faith and I are thinking—"

"It was to get away from her obnoxious neighbor."

"Bingo. We think maybe he threatened her and she realized she was in trouble. So she made a plan to get out of there. But he wasn't about to let her get away, not after all the fines the city imposed on him, and the police calls. Everything we've found on this guy supports him as a hothead who never let a perceived insult go unanswered. I've asked our law enforcement liaison to work with the police to get a subpoena for cell tower records. We need to prove whether he was near the victim's new home at the time of her murder. That'll take days. But we know for sure he wasn't at his house during that time. His whereabouts were unknown. He called in sick to work but his neighbors never saw him. And it sounds like they all kept tabs on him because they were afraid."

"Bottom line it for me, Asher."

"We believe this murder was the one that Raine used as her basis to build phony links to the other murders, as we've already figured out. I don't think she realized she may have actually stumbled onto a real killer. And it's sure looking as if she did."

"She performed surveillance on him," Callum said. "I remember reading that in the file."

"She did. Because of that, once Faith found the additional info early this morning, we sent a local PI to keep an eye on Scoggin. We want to make sure we know where he is at all times, just in case he saw Raine at any time and figured out who she was. If he thinks the cops are on to him—"

"He may blame her, or want to eliminate her as a potential witness. You said the PI is watching him?"

"He was. But Scoggin made him. He realized he had a tail and lost our guy. He's in the wind."

Callum's hand tightened around the phone. "What's his last known address?"

"Athens."

Callum drew his gun and sprinted for the stairs.

Chapter Fifteen

Raine shut off the shower and squeezed her hair to wring out the excess water. The bathroom door flew open. She gasped and jerked back as Callum ran inside. Gun in hand, pointed at the floor, he barely glanced at her and ran to the closet at the other end of the bathroom.

She grabbed the towel hanging over the top of the glass door and threw it around her, covering up just as he emerged. He'd put his gun away and was on the phone now.

"What's going on?" She stepped out of the shower onto the bath rug, clutching the towel against her body.

"It's okay," he silently mouthed, still on the phone. A second later, he was gone, the door closing behind him.

She should have been angry at the invasion of her privacy. But it was obvious that something was wrong. He'd come in here to make sure she was okay, and that no one else was with her. That much was obvious. What wasn't obvious was *why*. Why would she think someone else was up here? And who was he speaking to on the phone?

She hurriedly towel-dried her hair, not bothering with makeup. After throwing on a pair of jeans and a dark blue blouse, she stepped into her bedroom.

The first thing she noticed was that Callum was standing by one of the windows, peering through the plantation shutters toward the street out front. The second was that the wooden chair that normally sat at her reading desk was propped under the door handle on her bedroom door. No one was getting in, or out.

"Callum, good grief. What's going on? Why did you barge into the bathroom while I was naked, with your gun out?"

He flipped the shutters closed and walked over to her, his jaw set, worry lines creasing his brow. "To my credit, I did knock before going into the bathroom. And I called out your name, twice. You didn't answer."

"Yes, well, my head was probably under the water at the time. I didn't hear you."

"You've seen Pete Scoggin before. Describe him to me."

"Scoggin? What? Why?"

"Please."

She sighed. "Of course I've seen him. I performed surveillance on him. But I told you he had nothing to do with the murder cases I presented to you. It was all a fabrication to get your help."

"Not entirely." He leaned against the thick cherrywood post of her footboard. "You fabricated the alleged connection between Scoggin and the other murders you had in your files, presenting him as the serial killer we were searching for. But you were more right about him than you realized. It looks like he may very well have killed the first victim you looked into."

She pressed a hand to her chest. "Nancy Piraino? That was a guess more than anything, that he should be a suspect in her death. You really think he could be the one who murdered her?"

"It's looking that way. Faith and Asher dug into his background, and the victim's—"

"Nancy."

"Nancy. No one else in her life even remotely seems to have any reason to want to hurt her. Scoggin is the only one we've been able to find with both motive and opportunity."

She glanced at the chair under the door, her throat tightening. "And you think, what, that he's the one who broke into my home and tore it up? And that he might have gotten back in somehow?"

"The police are the ones who cleared the upstairs after I lost the suspect in the woods. Once I realized that the surveillance on Scoggin lost him, I had to make sure he hadn't managed to double back and sneak into the house again during the chaos."

She shivered and wrapped her arms around her waist. "Why would he come after me? Because he blames me for, what? Telling Unfinished Business about him? How would he even know I did that?"

"Not UB specifically. But you were watching him for a while. He may have noticed, took down your license plate number at some point, figured out who you were. We put out feelers to the police about him the same day we got your files. The police interviewed him that day, but had nothing to hold him on so they didn't arrest him. Now he's gone missing. No one knows where he is. He'd done some vandalism to Nancy's home at one point. I don't like that coincidence considering someone broke into your home and did the same. I haven't seen a picture of him yet. Can you describe him?"

She shrugged. "Nothing that really stands out. Shorter than you by several inches, probably about five-eight, five-nine. He wasn't heavy, average build I guess. Maybe even on the skinny side. Dark hair..." She drew a sharp breath. "I'm describing the same man we saw tonight."

He nodded. "You are." He pulled out his phone again and thumbed through some pictures, then held it up toward her. "Recognize this guy?"

"No, I... Wait. He's older, a little heavier, though not by much. Randy Hagen?"

"That's his most recent mug shot, from his latest drug arrest. Based on what you just said, he could be a double for Scoggin. Which means the guy I chased into the woods could be either one of them. If Hagen knows you've been nosing around and throwing his name into the mix to try to free your brother, he could have decided to try to scare you. I'm sure he wouldn't appreciate being labeled as a potential suspect, or accused of committing perjury at your brother's trial if it means he could get in trouble."

"He wouldn't be wrong. He could definitely get

in trouble." She climbed onto the foot of the bed and sat a few feet away from where he was leaning. "If he was proven to have perjured himself at trial, it wouldn't matter that the statute of limitations on perjury is only a few years. Here in Georgia, the clock doesn't start ticking on the limitations until the offense has been discovered. That means he could still be tried. And if convicted, since his false testimony sent someone to death row, he'd receive an automatic life sentence."

He whistled. "That's a hell of an incentive to want to keep you from talking to the police."

A sickening feeling shot through her, as if she'd just plunged down a steep incline. "Is he... Is either Scoggin or Hagen—"

"In the house? I don't believe so. But with you out of my sight up here, I had to make sure you were okay first. I didn't get a chance to search the whole house yet. We're not staying anyway, not with two men potentially close by with motives to want to hurt you."

"Not staying? You really think I'm in danger?"

"I'd rather overreact than assume you're safe here and be proven wrong. Your address is public knowledge. A simple internet search would find you. Someone already did."

She shivered and rubbed her arms. "Where can we go then? A hotel?"

"I want you somewhere safer than that, somewhere not out in public or easily found through an internet records search."

"Where would that be?"

Red and blue lights flashed across the shutters covering the windows.

He went to the nearest one and peered out. "I called Danny, Detective Cooper. He's going to put out a BOLO on Scoggin too, across Georgia and Tennessee, specifically for being wanted in connection with the murder of Nancy Piraino. It will be broadcast all over the media. We'll find him. I also asked Danny to send over one of the patrol officers he'd asked to watch the neighborhood. They're going to escort us, follow my SUV to make sure no one else follows us. We're going to a house where you'll be safe."

He crossed to the door, then moved the chair out from under the doorknob. "I'll let him know you'll be down in a few minutes. Pack a bag. We'll leave as soon as you're ready."

"Callum, wait. Where are we going? What house are you talking about where you think I'll be safe?"

He paused in the doorway and looked back at her. "Mine."

Chapter·Sixteen

They headed east on State Road 78, which Raine knew better as Lexington Road. Behind them, the police car followed, keeping an eye out to ensure that no one else followed them. Not long after passing the airport, Lexington became Athens Road, but still Callum showed no signs of slowing or making any turns.

"You said I should go someplace where no one would know to look," she said. "If someone, say Hagen, hears that we were asking questions around town, he might know to look for your place in case I went there with you."

"Good thinking, counselor. But the property deed, even the utilities, aren't registered under my name. They're under a maze of shell corporations. I did that back when I received some threats as a detective with ACCPD. I didn't want any bad guys I'd put away to find out where I lived. When I moved to Gatlinburg, I did the same there. Neither home will come back to me unless someone does an incredible amount of digging. And even then, when they pull records to figure out who's behind each corporation, I'd find out. I bribed a city clerk to flag my file so that if anyone ever requested the information, I'd be notified."

"That explains why I never could find your address when I was internet stalking you."

He grinned. "Good to know my precautions worked."

"The curiosity is killing me. How much farther is this shell-corporation-owned place?"

"Another ten minutes or so. It was an aggravatingly long drive to and from work back in the day. Now that I live in Gatlinburg, I rarely make it out here. The last time was months ago, when I took a handful of days off between cases."

"Must be an awfully nice place to have made your long commute worth it, and to keep it even after you moved to Tennessee."

He smiled. "Emphasis on *awful*. The house is small and plain, nothing to brag about. It's the property that's nice. A wooded oasis not too far from city amenities but isolated enough so that no one knows your business. It was my grandfather's, on my dad's side of the family. He willed it to me when he passed away. I'd just turned eighteen."

"Eighteen, wow. Young to become a landowner. You keep it for sentimental reasons?"

"More like I keep it to tick off my family. They were furious that Granddad willed it to me instead of my dad. My parents and siblings tried to get me to sell it and split the proceeds. I refused, on principle mostly. My grandfather didn't want it sold. If my dad had planned on keeping it, I'd have signed it right over. But all he wanted to do was sell to a developer to split into parcels and build a subdivision." He glanced at her. "That family tension went on for years, getting worse over time. Family gatherings were a study in walking on eggshells to avoid arguments. After a particularly uncomfortable visit, with everyone again trying to get me to sell and me refusing, my family decided I was being greedy and pretty much shunned me. That was five years ago."

"That's truly awful. Is there a reason they were so pushy about your property? Like maybe they were hurting for money and wanted the proceeds?"

"If that was the case, I'd have sold immediately. No one in my family is wealthy. But we're not hurting by any means. All of us have good-paying jobs. And my parents made enough after selling their small chain of office-supply stores to a big-box retailer to retire early."

"I'm so sorry they treated you like that. Possessions should never come between people who are supposed to love each other."

"Don't be sorry. I get along fine on my own."

"You shouldn't have to though. As your family, they should love you unconditionally."

His Adam's apple bobbed in his throat but he didn't reply.

The flash of pain she'd seen in his eyes told her far more than his flippant words and matter-of-fact demeanor. Unable to resist the impulse, she put her left hand over his right hand that was resting on the console between them.

His gaze shot to hers in surprise. Then he surprised *her* by turning his hand palm up and threading their fingers together.

"Thanks, Raine." His deep voice sent a warm thrill up her spine as his hand tightened on hers. "If anyone knows about loyalty and unconditional love, it's you. That's one of the things I admire about you."

She blinked. "You admire me? The woman who held you at gunpoint?"

He laughed, the stress lines in his brow easing. "Not the most auspicious of first-meets, for sure. But I get it now. I understand why you did it. And the fact that you did, knowing the gun wasn't loaded and putting your own life at risk to make sure you didn't hurt an innocent person, well, that's far more telling about your character than anything else. You're a good person, Raine Quintero. Even if you are a lawyer."

She rolled her eyes and tugged her hand free, more because she was tempted to scoot closer than because she was upset. "I'm not sure if that was a compliment or an insult."

"A little of both. My apologies." He winked.

Her face warmed and she blew out a shaky breath. Callum was a charmer. If she wasn't careful, she was going to fall for the cop partly responsible for her brother being in prison—on death row, no less. That wasn't family loyalty. That was the complete opposite. Her brother would be ashamed of her, and hurt. Which had a world of guilt crashing down on her. Here he was, counting down the few remaining days of his life in a six-by-nine cell, and she was flirting instead of working to free him. She kind of hated herself in that moment.

"What's the plan now?" she asked. "Once we get to your place."

He gave her a questioning look, no doubt wondering at her sudden mood change. But he took it in stride, casually moving the hand that had held hers onto the steering wheel as he drove them farther away from town.

"First, I'll put in an order to a delivery service to drop off some groceries, come morning. I've got a refrigerator in the carport where they can put it if we're not there when they arrive. For tonight, we'll survive on whatever I've got in the freezer."

"I meant what are we going to do next to help my brother. It's getting late. I know we can't do much more tonight. But you work cold cases all the time. You must have some kind of game plan for approaching them aside from visiting the crime scene."

He put on his left blinker and slowed to a stop, waiting for the headlights of an oncoming car to pass and rolling down his window. As soon as the car went by, he turned left onto a narrow dirt-and-gravel road surrounded by thick trees illuminated by his headlights. He waved out the window. Raine looked over her shoulder to see the cop car turning around in the middle of the road. Then he headed back toward town.

"The policeman isn't coming with us down this street?" she asked.

"No need. It's my driveway."

She straightened in surprise and looked around—or tried. It was too dark to see much. The tree branches overhead blocked out the moonlight. And there weren't any spotlights anywhere on the property.

Until he made one last turn.

"Oh, wow," she breathed.

He chuckled. "And now you see why my grandfather loved this place so much."

He pulled to a stop about twenty yards from the small white concrete block ranch home that sat off to their right. Raine barely spared it a glance. What had her attention was the play of landscaping lights all across the yard, both front and back. Except that it wasn't so much a yard as manicured land with gorgeous groupings of ornamental trees and plants, illuminated by sparkling white lights.

Woven amongst the plantings was a stone walkway that went all the way to the sparkling water beyond. The pond didn't seem to be very large, although in the daylight it might be bigger than she thought. A fountain splashed in the middle, lit by a ring of floating spotlights. And a short dock that looked more suited to sitting and relaxing than launching any kind of small boat stuck out just a few short yards into the water, with ornamental lamp posts on each end.

"It's incredible. Beautiful. I'll bet you sit on that

dock for hours when you come up here. It's a perfect reading spot."

"I hadn't thought of that before. Reading isn't something I get much time to do outside of work. But it's a great place to fish, or just unwind, drink a beer and pretend the rest of the world doesn't exist."

"How does it stay this nice? You said you don't get up here much."

"Not enough to keep up the property, for sure. It costs a small fortune to have a landscaping company maintain it. But every time I think about stopping the expense, letting nature take over, I remember my grandma out here on her hands and knees tending to all the beds. She and Granddad planted almost every plant, every bush, every tree out here. I helped weed and water and clear areas for new beddings more times than I can count. Letting it go feels like, I don't know, like letting *them* go I suppose. Seems silly, but—"

"Not at all. You honor them and their memory by keeping this place up. It's a living memorial to their lives and their love for you. Destroying this, mowing it all down to build cookie-cutter homes, would be a travesty. Your family doesn't deserve this property if they can't appreciate it."

When it finally dawned on her that he'd been silent for some time, she tore her gaze away from the fantasyland outside the windows and found him intently watching her. Under the light of the moon, the dash and the twinkling landscape lights in the distance, everything suddenly seemed…magical, full of possibilities. The stress, the unknowns, her worries about the investigation faded away as he slowly unclipped his seat belt, all while capturing her gaze with his.

Somehow, she managed to unbuckle hers as well, and then they were in each other's arms. Like the magician she now knew him to be, he wrapped her in an achingly sweet embrace and pressed his lips to hers. Briefly, far too briefly. But oh so wonderful. Then his lips moved to the column of her throat, making her gasp from the heat.

He groaned deep in his throat and half turned, pressing her against the back of the seat. This time, when his lips captured hers, there was nothing brief about it. He took his time, making love to her mouth with his, caressing, stroking, giving and taking until she wanted to weep from the beauty of it.

When he finally pulled back, he gently stroked her hair, moving her bangs back from her eyes.

"That was…beautiful," she whispered. "I've never been kissed like that before."

"That's a shame," he whispered back. "You should be kissed like that thoroughly, and often. Treasured and cherished."

"Careful. You may be ruining me for others."

He smiled, his warm hands blazing a trail down the sides of her face to her neck, her shoulders. "Is that what I'm doing? Ruining you for others?" He pressed a tender kiss against her collarbone.

She shivered. "What others?"

He chuckled, his hot breath making her shiver again before he pulled back. "Sadly, we have to stop, or I'm going to make love to you right here in the cab of my SUV. And you deserve much better than that. Let's get inside the house."

He drove into the carport, and just like that, the brain cells that had deserted Raine came rushing back. Make love? What the heck was she thinking to even want him to do that? Because she did. She wanted him, more than she'd ever wanted anyone. And she didn't understand it. Yes, he was handsome, incredibly so. And strong, and gentle, and smart, and…and he was the investigator working her brother's case. No matter how much she longed to be in his arms, that had to take a back seat to what truly mattered.

Saving Joey's life.

Her door opened and Callum was standing there holding the bag she'd packed, his smile fading as he watched her grab her purse.

"The moment's gone, isn't it?" His tone dripped with regret. "I gave you too much time to think."

"It's a good thing you did. We have to stay focused on what matters."

He stared at her a long moment, then nodded as if coming to some kind of understanding. "What matters. Absolutely. I should have known better. It won't happen again."

As he started to turn away, she tossed her purse to the floor and grabbed his hand. "Callum, wait."

He turned around, his brows arched in question. She reached for him and pulled him closer, then framed his face with her hands. She pressed a whisper-soft kiss against his lips, then stared up into his eyes.

"I'm sorry. I didn't mean that the way it sounded. What we just did, who you are, matters. But it's so unexpected, surprising, because we barely know each other. And I'm not sure how to even deal with this…thing that's happening between us right now. I'm struggling just to hold myself together, knowing that my brother is going to die in a matter of days if I don't pull some kind of miracle out of my hat. I need to focus on that right now, instead of losing myself in you, even though I so desperately want to. I'm not making much sense, I know, but can you understand that? A little? You do matter, Callum. You matter a great deal to me. Somehow. Impossibly, in such a short time. But there it is. Truth."

He smiled as he gently pushed her hair back again. "You're full of surprises, Raine Quintero. And I do understand what you're saying. Leave it to the lawyer to make a strong argument. But I don't agree with the premise. I think you can mix business and pleasure. And I've learned that sometimes *not* thinking about a problem a hundred percent of the time helps me focus better when I come back to that problem."

"Are you arguing that making love will help us focus better, Callum?"

His smile broadened. "Would it get you into my bed if I were?"

She laughed. "No. We have work to do. And no time to waste." She held up a hand. "Not waste. Time to spend on other things that are no doubt pleasurable—"

"Hot, wonderful, mind-blowing—"

She laughed. "We need to work on this lack of confidence of yours."

"I'm at your service, whenever you're ready."

"Good grief." She fanned herself. "You're incorrigible."

"And stopping, right now. I'm honestly not trying to change your mind. I respect your decision. Let's get inside and I'll answer your earlier question."

He headed to the side door and fit his key in the lock.

She grabbed her purse and hurried after him as the door swung open. "My earlier question?"

"You wanted to know my plans for solving your brother's cold case."

She blinked. "Right. Your plans. See what I mean? You distracted me."

"The pleasure was all mine, I assure you. But I'll try to be good from here on out."

She shook her head in exasperation. This man was a rascal, irresistible. He kept saying she was a surprise. Well, he was even more of a surprise to her. Not at all what she'd expected. He was rapidly becoming everything she never realized she wanted. But if she gave in to her longings now, and they couldn't save her brother, would she ever be able to forgive herself? Or him? That wasn't the kind of guilt she wanted to contemplate. Which meant any kind of a relationship between her and Callum wasn't possible, not now. And depending on what happened to Joey, maybe not ever.

Chapter Seventeen

Raine's request to know Callum's plans for pursuing her brother's case still had her head spinning the next afternoon as they headed to yet another appointment. What had surprised her the most as he went through the list of things being done in the investigation was that he had several people at his company, Unfinished Business, helping. She hadn't even realized that. She thought everyone was working other cases or the serial killer one. But apparently they approached all of their cases as a team, sharing resources as needed, especially with something as critical as trying to beat the ticking clock of an upcoming execution.

Team members had been validating information from the trial transcripts and police files. They'd been working on that since the moment she'd handed over her printed files and computer, even before she'd been released from the hospital.

UB had its own in-house lab. One of its analysts was reviewing the physical evidence from the case, or at least the inventory list of it in the police files.

They were examining the reports on the forensic testing that had been done to see whether they felt other evidence should also be tested. Of course, if they wanted additional tests, there would have to be a strong argument to get the prosecution to even allow them access. And that kind of testing took time, time Joey didn't have. Raine wasn't holding out much hope on the forensics front. But she deeply appreciated them looking, just the same. Miracles happened. She only needed one.

Key witness testimony had been read and was being compared with written reports by the prosecution and defense. Callum had explained that was to ensure all discovery rules had been followed. If any evidence hadn't been properly turned over to the defense before trial, that could be used to argue that the trial was unfair. But, again, Raine doubted that strategy would result in anything. It was an obvious one that should have been found out years ago if discovery rules had been violated.

Her hopes really hinged on the interviews, both with witnesses who'd testified and others who hadn't. If someone recanted their testimony, or substantially changed it from what they'd originally said, that could be used to argue an unfair trial. It would be looked at as new evidence, which was what they desperately needed. She was really hoping that Callum or his peers could come up with new witnesses who could completely call Joey's guilt into doubt. The board couldn't ignore evidence like that. They would have to act, even if only to temporarily put a halt to the execution.

UB's investigators were also conducting searches on various law enforcement databases, looking for similar crimes much as she'd done, but with access to data she couldn't get.

Experts were being consulted on all kinds of things. And UB lawyers were looking into the appeals that had been done on Joey's behalf, searching for loopholes and opportunities that may have been previously overlooked.

And that was just what Raine could remember from last night's discussion. At one point, she'd begged for mercy. And she'd apologized for even questioning him. Obviously, the UB investigators—especially Callum—knew what they were doing. Her worries that she and Callum weren't working hard enough to make a dent were completely unfounded. People were working the case around the clock. Dozens of avenues were being explored. But of course, even knowing that, she couldn't afford for her or Callum to slow down.

He was the boots on the ground, their expert in Athens. He was the one who could speak to people in person, push for an interview that may have been refused over the phone to someone at UB in Gatlinburg. What she and Callum did could result in the one little piece of information that would tip the board in their favor. They had to keep going. Which was why—after spending hours already today talking to witnesses—they were now on the campus of the University of Georgia.

Over half an hour earlier, an administrator had led them to a criminal justice studies waiting area outside the office of Professor Irena Kassin—expert on the phenomenon of false confessions. They had an appointment but the time had come and gone. Apparently the wheels of justice moved slowly even on a college campus.

Callum had already cautioned Raine not to get her hopes up with any of these interviews. But he'd especially warned her about this upcoming one. The idea that Joey's confession may have been coerced wasn't new. It was the basic argument in many of his lawyer's court proceedings over the years. For it to be argued again, successfully this time, they'd have to come up with some extremely compelling evidence.

So far, in spite of all of their hard work and the full resources of UB at their disposal, they had nothing. That was why, in spite of Callum's warnings, Raine was putting her hopes on this professor. Her credentials were impeccable. She'd not only written several books about false confessions, she'd conducted numerous scientific studies on it. And she'd testified in over fifty cases. What impressed Raine the most about that number was that she'd testified almost equally for the defense and the prosecution. Looking at her record, no one could accuse her of bias one way or the other. If she was convinced that Joey's confession was bogus, that had to carry weight with the prison board. It *had* to.

The door to Professor Kassin's office finally opened. A man in a dark-colored business suit came out, nodded at them and left. The young admin headed into the office. A moment later she emerged and motioned for them to go in.

Raine wasn't sure what she'd expected of a criminal justice professor with several books and nationally acclaimed studies on her résumé. But it certainly wasn't the fashion-forward beautiful brunette who greeted them. She seemed to smile more warmly at Callum, hold his hand perhaps a little longer than necessary as they exchanged pleasantries. It was all Raine could manage not to knock the woman's hand away. And wasn't that ridiculous? One kiss. She and Callum had shared one kiss. She shouldn't be feeling like she wanted to claw another woman's eyes out just because she smiled at him.

But dang it, she did.

Thankfully, her uncharacteristic jealousy quickly faded as the professor began to educate them about the science behind the study of false confessions. Instead, Raine became engrossed in the depth of Kassin's knowledge. And impressed that she'd spent several hours this morning preparing for their interview. She'd studied the police reports on Joey's alleged confession that UB had provided. And she'd also managed to read through parts of the trial transcript, at least the ones relevant to his interrogation. She must have spent half her day preparing to speak to them. That alone had Raine feeling guilty for her silly jealousy, and overwhelmingly grateful.

Kassin smiled from behind her desk. "I know I've thrown a lot at you in a short amount of time. The amount of information out there on the false-confession phenomenon can be overwhelming. I'll summarize some of the main points, and try to relate it back to Mr. Quintero's specific situation."

Behind her desk, she flipped through some notes on a yellow legal pad. She ran a long red fingernail across several items, then nodded as if to assure herself about what she'd written. Smiling again, she tapped the first bullet point and sat back in her chair.

"I'll try to frame things with some statistics. It should help to paint a better picture of what we've been discussing. The statistics come from cases where a conviction was overturned due to new evidence. This gives us a pool of cases to study where we know an innocent person was wrongly convicted. When we examine those wrongful convictions, we find that false confessions—where a suspect says they committed the crime even though they didn't—are the leading cause of those convictions in homicide cases. Shocking, isn't it?"

"Not to me," Raine said. "My brother is walking proof."

"I'll admit it's a surprise on my part," Callum said. "I've never heard it stated that way and honestly didn't expect it."

Kassin nodded. "It gets worse. When examining cases—not just homicides—that were overturned as a result of the work done by various innocence groups, we find that anywhere from twenty-five percent to sixty-six percent of them involved false confessions. Extrapolating that out, one can conclude that fifty thousand or more innocent people are in prison right now, just in this country alone, because they confessed to a crime they didn't commit. That is a staggeringly high amount. And it points to a major flaw in our judicial system."

Raine was stunned at the percentages the professor had just quoted.

Callum seemed equally surprised. He leaned forward in his chair and rested his elbows on his knees. "Assuming all of those figures you quoted are accurate—"

"They are," Kassin assured him.

He smiled. "What I can't understand is how it happens in the first place. No one could make me confess to something I didn't do, especially not murder."

"And that, Mr. Wright, is the problem. People don't understand how it can happen. Therefore, they automatically assume it doesn't. But since we can prove it does happen, with an alarming frequency, we need to understand how and why it occurs. And then we need to retrain law enforcement and prosecutors to recognize it and prevent it. Interrogation techniques at the very least need to change."

Callum sat back and crossed his arms. "If you're going to argue that detectives should follow a whole new set of rules and play nice, you'll never get support for that. You can't tie the hands of the good guys when working with criminals who have no morals and no rules. We'd never convict anyone if that was the case."

"I disagree. But more importantly, your argument nicely illustrates one of the main issues involved in false confessions. Detectives assume people are guilty when they interview them. The whole no-morals-and-no-rules thing implies they're criminals and that they must have committed the offense about which they are being interviewed. That's a bias going into the interrogation that automatically skews things against the suspect."

Callum shook his head, clearly displeased. "Innocent until proven guilty guides the jury in a court of law. If detectives never believed someone was guilty, they'd never make an arrest or interrogate them in the first place."

Kassin nodded. "I agree with you on that last point. It's a dilemma. As for changing up how interrogations are conducted, that's something that has to be explored or we'll never solve the problem of false confessions. But you're not here to solve that problem. You and Ms. Quintero are here to understand the problem, and how it may or may not relate to her brother's situation."

She sat forward and addressed her next comments to Raine. "There are many factors that can lead to someone saying they committed a crime even when they didn't. Being overly tired, or mentally challenged in some way, or even under the influence of some kind of substance makes the suspect vulnerable to suggestion."

Callum was the focus of her next comments. "Police interrogation techniques have a huge impact, as you might imagine. Law enforcement is trained to use psychology that, unfortunately, can influence anyone—guilty or not. That includes isolating a suspect in an uncomfortable room with few amenities. The environment is unfamiliar and makes the suspect nervous, unsure. Interviewers wield all the power. They barrage suspects by accusing them of being guilty, over and over."

"Sounds like brainwashing," Raine said.

Callum shot her an aggravated glance.

"That's a good way to describe it," the professor agreed. "Imagine yourself in a room for hours, feeling helpless, powerless. You're tired, confused and being told you're a bad person by the people in charge with all the power. Then one of them may play good cop, commiserate with you, try to give you an out—an excuse for your behavior. If the suspect denies their guilt, the investigator often interrupts them and tells them they're guilty. They'll provide a counterpoint, arguments to discredit any facts the suspect may present. Again, psychology is huge here. The interviewers won't allow the suspect to go quiet. They keep them talking so they can't stop and calm down and think about what they're saying."

"I never conducted my interviews that way," Callum protested.

"That's commendable," she said. "Have you ever lied to a suspect? Acted polite and as if you're their friend? Encouraged them to get it off their chest and everything will be okay?"

He sat back, quiet.

"Your silence tells me you have," she said. "And I'm not saying there's necessarily anything wrong with that, in and of itself. But if you combine that, gaining the suspect's trust, and they are already vulnerable, such as through mental defect, they may tell you what they think you want to hear. And they'll do that thinking they're pleasing you, and that once they make you happy you'll let them go home."

He shook his head. "No one is going to confess to murder and think they're going to get to go home afterward."

"I can show you files from dozens of cases that prove otherwise."

The look on Callum's face had Raine worried that this was going to devolve into a heated debate. That wasn't going to help Joey.

"Hold it," Raine said. "Can we please get back on track? Let's not argue about this. We're here to learn, to see whether Professor Kassin thinks Joey's confession was coerced."

Callum blew out a deep breath. "My apologies to both of you. I was a junior detective when I worked on Joey's case and this is hitting a little close to home."

Kassin's eyes widened. "I don't recall seeing your name in the file as one of the interrogators."

"Perhaps junior detective is too generous." A wry grin twisted his lips. "Detective Farley was the lead on the case. He interviewed Joey. I was his gopher. But the idea that something untoward could have gone on while I was working there bugs me. If I believed Farley was coercing any innocent people into lying, I assure you I'd have put a stop to it somehow."

Raine touched his shoulder to get his attention. "I've learned enough about you to know, one hundred percent, that you would never knowingly do anything to impinge on a suspect's rights or try to get a confession at all costs."

His look of surprise had her feeling even worse about how she'd first met him. He was a man of character and she never should have taken his choice away from him about helping her. Instead, she should have tried harder to get an audience with him and let him choose whether or not he wanted to help.

The professor flipped a page on her legal pad, no doubt her unsubtle way of regaining their attention. "The last part I'll add is that length of time of an interrogation comes into play. The longer it goes on, the more a suspect is likely to lie just to make it end. The younger a suspect is, as well, the more vulnerable he or she is." She flipped another page. "Regarding Joey's interviews, there were several things that concerned me."

One by one, she listed potential problems with his interviews, especially the last one, where he supposedly confessed.

"The interviews were long. Joey expressed he was suffering from insomnia, so he was already tired.

There was no recording, either audio or visual, of the interviews. The printed confession that Joey signed has phrasing and word choices that never appear in other samples of his writing that his lawyer included in his file. In short, when I review everything in its entirety, there are some red flags. I have concerns about whether he was unduly influenced or coerced to sign a write-up of the confession that didn't accurately reflect what he said."

Raine stared at her, frozen, afraid to hope, afraid to even breathe. "I don't... I'm not sure what to do with that. Are you saying...are you saying in your expert opinion that—"

The look of empathy on the professor's face had Raine clutching a hand to her chest.

Don't say it. Don't say it. Don't—

"Ms. Quintero, there are definitely parts of your brother's interrogations that concern me. But looking at everything in total, at all of his interviews and how they were handled, there's nothing there that I can absolutely point to and say his confession was coerced."

Barely aware that Callum had placed a supportive hand on her shoulder, she stared in shock at the other woman. "I don't understand. You said there are red flags. You have concerns. You can speak to the board and—"

"What I can do, and will do, is offer a critique and recommendations to ACCPD for future interrogations. As for speaking to the prison board on

Mr. Quintero's behalf, I can't in good conscience do that. I'm sorry, Ms. Quintero. But there's nothing I can do to help your brother."

Chapter Eighteen

Once Raine had recovered from Professor Kassin's devastating conclusions—or lack of conclusions— she'd put her brave face back on and accompanied Callum on dozens of other interviews. But here it was, more than a week later, and in spite of how incredibly hard he was working, the lack of sleep, the endless hours he spent poring over files in his home office, they weren't any closer to saving Joey.

And time was their enemy.

It hit her hard, during breakfast on Callum's back patio earlier this morning, that the next handful of days could very well be her brother's last. And here she was, in Callum's SUV now, watching the landscape roll past the window while he drove them to yet another interview.

She'd spent this precious time talking to strangers, driving countless miles, with nothing to show for it. Was there some point at which she should stop, give up? Should she instead go see her brother, take advantage of the lax visiting rules as his execution date drew near? Did it make more sense to talk to him through a thick pane of glass and an old-fashioned phone, with nothing new to share, no hope to give him? Or was her time better spent in the seemingly endless conference calls with his lawyers? And brainstorming with Callum. No matter what she did, it didn't seem as if it even mattered anymore.

A single tear spilled over her lashes and ran down her cheek. She quickly wiped it away and drew a ragged breath.

Callum's warm, strong hand was suddenly on top of hers. She automatically threaded her fingers with his and took the comfort he offered. They'd become so used to each other's moods that they often didn't even have to say anything to understand what the other was thinking, feeling. It was a closeness she treasured and relied on so much now that she didn't know how she'd survive without his support going forward. Here she was, the hardened lawyer who'd spent most of her adult life fighting for justice in one way or another. And yet, when it really mattered, she was losing the battle and thinking about giving up.

"Don't give up yet, Raine. We're not done. Not even close." He squeezed her hand.

Her throat tightened. It was as if he'd read her thoughts. Again. Somehow, when she was at her lowest, he always knew what to say, and how to make her feel better. Just knowing he hadn't given up gave her the strength to straighten in her seat and sniff back the tears.

When she trusted her voice again to be able to speak, she asked, "How is the serial killer investigation going? You haven't given me any updates lately, except to say no new victims have been discovered. Maybe the killer died. Or he was sent to prison on some other charge. Wouldn't that be a blessing?"

"If it meant he'd never be out on the streets again, hurting anyone else, it sure would be. But the families of his victims need closure, if that even exists. At the very least, they need to *know* the man who hurt their loved ones is locked away for good. I did speak to Asher this morning, when you were taking your shower. The team has zeroed in on a suspect. Ever hear of a guy named Drake Knox when you were looking into the case?"

"Drake Knox." She thought a moment, then shook her head. "Doesn't ring a bell. Who is he?"

"Someone who would never appear on the police radar. He's a trust fund baby, living off his inherited wealth. Never worked a day in his life, doesn't have to. No criminal record. No history, that we know of, of animal abuse or other warning signs typical of someone who goes on to become a serial killer. Then again, he was an only child, raised in the family mansion on property up in the Smoky Mountains, somewhat isolated. He was homeschooled, not that it's a precursor or cause of psychopathic tendencies. But it paints a picture of him growing up pretty much alone, with only his parents or nannies to socialize him."

"If he's so antitypical and isn't on police radar, why does UB think he's the killer you've been looking for?"

"Asher isn't sure he's the killer, not yet. He's just the only viable suspect they've come up with, so they're looking deeply into his past and trying to form timelines for where he might have been during the killings. His name originally came up as someone in the area during the same time frame as two of the murders. There have been few links between any of the victims. They've been pretty random. So to find someone who was in the social circle, for a brief time at least, of two victims got Asher and Faith curious about him. So far, they've linked him to an additional victim as far as timelines go and being in the area when the murder happened. That's a total of three, and they're still looking for more links."

"Sounds promising. I hope they're onto something."

"There is one more thing that makes Knox look promising. Four of the victims' cars were found to have illegal GPS trackers on them, attached to the frame. Knox was pulled over in a traffic stop once, years ago, and one of the things the cop noted on the ticket was that Knox had GPS tracking equipment sitting on the seat beside him. He thought it was odd enough to put it in his write-up."

"That's really odd. How did he explain it? Knox?"

"He didn't. He told the cop it was none of his business what he had in his car. And since it was a simple traffic stop, he's right. The officer didn't have any just cause to do a search. But obviously it raises flags. A theory we've always had about the victims is that they were stalked for some time before being killed. That's based on the fact that these women had busy lives and he always managed to get to them when they were alone, like when their boyfriends in two of those cases were gone on business trips. A GPS tracker would make following them easy."

He squeezed her hand again. "Enough about that. Let's focus on Joey's case. You don't have to go on all of these interviews with me. If you don't feel up to it today, I can—"

"Don't tell me to go home now. I'd never forgive myself if we can't... If we're unable to stop... If I didn't do everything I could for my brother. You never know. I could think of the one question in an interview that might shake some new information loose. Or I could connect the dots in a different way than you and come up with a new avenue to explore. I want to be there."

"Fair enough. I spoke to Danny, Detective Cooper, this morning too. The BOLOs are still out on Scoggin and Hagen. No sightings of either of them. UB is actively researching Scoggin to try to find him, see if he's a one-off killer or whether Knox could be responsible for that one too. Danny did finally finish evaluating the cases that Farley worked."

As he passed a slow-moving car, she said, "I'm guessing from your tone this is going to be another disappointment."

He nodded. "There aren't any patterns to show that Farley purposely chose to not record confessions and recorded other, non-confession interviews. Danny even reviewed the data with Internal Affairs to make sure he wasn't missing anything. They agreed with him. There's no basis to think Farley was anything other than lazy or inept about being consistent with recording interviews. And like Professor Kassin, IA doesn't feel there's enough evidence in the written transcripts of Joey's confession to argue it was coerced. I'm sorry, Raine. I wish I had better news."

She tugged her hand free and wrapped her arms around her middle as she looked out the window. "Not your fault. You're doing everything humanly possible, as well as half the team at UB."

"Half is stretching it. They've had to move resources to dig into the Knox angle and follow up on Scoggin too. But if we have anything we need help with, we can get some local PIs in on it."

"I understand." And she did. UB had many cases to focus on. Expending most of their resources to help her with a closed case, when they were working on a cold case that had heated up, didn't make sense. If she was the owner of UB, she'd have reallocated resources too. But that didn't mean it didn't sink her hopes even lower.

"Four days," she whispered brokenly. "They're going to kill him in four days."

"Not if we can stop it. I told you, don't give up yet. I made an appointment with Joey's lawyers and the prison board for the morning of his scheduled execution date. We'll present whatever we've found. They'll rule on it right after the meeting, granting a stay if they feel they need more time."

"Well, that's something. That's a good thing."

"It is," he agreed as he slowed and turned into an apartment complex.

"Thank you, Callum. For everything. I don't know how I would have gotten through all of this without you. Truly."

"My pleasure. Now, stop moping around and engage that amazing brain of yours. We're about to conduct another interview."

He parked in front of the first apartment building on the left. Then he leaned over and pressed a whisper-soft kiss against her lips, then quickly pulled back. "Oops. Couldn't help it." He winked, making a lie out of his apology.

She laughed, unable to resist his charm, as always. "I'll forgive you this once."

He grinned and they both got out of the SUV.

Regret gnawed at Raine once they were sitting on a couch across from the woman who lived in apartment 1101. Her name was Rose Garcia and she'd dated Joey for two years. And yet, Raine had only met her a few times. Rose had testified as a character witness at Joey's trial, on behalf of the defense. But Raine barely knew her. She and Joey had been like ships passing in the night, partly because he was so much older than her. It was only after his arrest, and conviction, that she'd made the efforts she should have made earlier. Their age gap should never have been an excuse to not be involved in her brother's life. It was one of many regrets she had to live with.

"Rose, we appreciate your time," Callum said.

"And you've been very helpful in telling us Joey's usual routines, where he liked to go, people he considered his friends. Now, I'd like you to focus on the day that Alicia Claremont was murdered. The prosecution's timeline indicated that there was a three-hour window in which Joey could have killed her. Is there any additional information about that day that you've remembered that can help us flesh out the timeline, narrow that window of opportunity? Perhaps you have something written down that might jog your memory, a diary, or journal? Maybe an old calendar you saved that has appointments and notes on it about Joey? Documents with dates in particular could really help. Lawyers love those as evidence."

Rose twisted her hands in her lap, her gaze darting around the worn, beige-colored room. "I testified at his trial. I told them he was a good person."

Callum glanced at Raine before continuing. "Are you worried about telling us something different than what you said under oath?"

She twisted her hands even harder, her knuckles whitening.

Raine scooted forward on the couch. "Rose? Can you look at me, please?" She kept her voice soft, as unthreatening and nonjudgmental as possible.

Finally Rose met her gaze. "You're Joey's sister."

She smiled sadly, her stomach dropping at the implications in Rose's hesitation, her demeanor and her worry over Raine being his sister. "It's okay to tell the truth, whatever it is. That's exactly what we want, no matter what. No one's going to get upset at you."

Rose chewed her bottom lip and looked down at her hands.

Callum gave Rose a sympathetic look. "Would it be easier to talk if Raine leaves the room?"

Still, Rose remained silent.

Raine stood. "I'll wait in the car."

"No." Rose sighed heavily and stood. "Have a seat. Please. If you really want the truth, then you deserve to hear it. Give me a minute." She headed down the short hallway and disappeared into what Raine assumed was her bedroom.

Callum's hand covered hers. "Are you sure you want to be here for whatever she's going to say?"

"Yes. As she said, I want the truth."

He studied her for a long moment, then nodded and pulled his hand back.

Rose emerged from her room and returned to her spot in the recliner across from them. In her hands was a blue spiral-bound notebook, the kind you could get for a few dollars at a convenience store. But from the worn look of it and dog-eared pages, she'd had it a long time.

As she placed it on the glass coffee table between them and flipped it open, Raine couldn't help but tense. The word *DIARY* was spelled out in block letters across the top, along with a date—two months prior to Alicia's murder.

The woman's hands shook as she flipped through the pages, stopping at the first one written in red ink instead of the blue that had been used on other pages. The date, again, was at the top—six weeks before Joey's trial. A legal-sized envelope was nestled against the opposite page. Rose took it out and set it on the coffee table. But instead of opening it, she flipped to the end of the journal.

Another envelope lay there, this one much thicker than the first. Written in blue ink across it was one word—*trial*. She handed the envelope to Callum.

"You want me to open this?" he asked.

She nodded. "Please. You can show Raine too. I think she's seen most of them before."

And she had. As Callum thumbed through them, leaning close to Raine so she could see them too, she recognized them as having been entered into evidence at trial. Or, at least, copies of these photos. She didn't think very much of the evidence had been released, not while there was still a chance of another trial, no matter how remote.

"We were happy then," Rose said. "Good times."

Callum stopped thumbing through the pictures. "Not all the times were good?"

Rose's cheeks turned a light pink as she glanced at Raine. She cleared her throat. "No. They weren't." She picked up the first envelope that obviously contained more photos and handed it to him.

As soon as he pulled out the first picture, Raine gasped and pressed a hand to her throat. It was a selfie of Rose, standing in front of a bathroom mirror. Her throat had purplish bruises on it. Even without being a forensic expert, Raine could easily tell what had made those bruises. Hands.

"Rose?" Callum asked, his voice soft. "Who did this to you?"

Her eyes brightened with unshed tears. "My sweet Joey. I don't even remember what I did to make him mad." She twisted her hands and looking imploringly at Raine. "I didn't lie about him being sweet at the trial. I wanted people to know he was a good person. He was sweet, kind, smart. He took good care of me...when he was sober. I just...didn't tell them about when he wasn't sober."

Raine fought back her own tears as Callum flipped through the other pictures. When he was through, he put them in the envelope and slid them across the table.

"Those are some awful injuries," he said, his voice still kind, gentle. "Are you saying Joey was responsible for all of them?"

She nodded. "But only because he was drunk, or sometimes high. I loved him. Still do. But that last time, the throat, he choked me. I passed out. When I woke up, he went white as a sheet, as if he'd seen a ghost. I'm pretty sure he thought he'd killed me." She wiped her eyes, refusing to let the tears fall. "I don't know why I took those pictures, or why I kept them. I guess it was my subconscious, wanting proof for later, when I was in denial. Countless nights, after he'd been out drinking, I'd sit in my room, waiting for him to come home. Wondering if tonight would be one of those nights. I think...those pictures, seeing how many there were, are what finally gave me the courage to leave him."

"I'm so sorry," Raine whispered. "So sorry."

Rose shook her head. "Don't be. It's not your fault. It wasn't Joey's either, not really. Alcohol released a monster inside him. He never would have done it if he was in his right mind. He loved me."

Raine exchanged an agonized glance with Callum. They didn't have to speak for her to know that he was remembering the same thing she was—the police report for when Joey was arrested. Although sober by the time they found him, he reeked of alcohol and had bloodshot eyes, indicating a recent binge.

"I don't doubt you, Rose. But for this to be evidence, we need proof. Do you have anything to show that Joey is the one who did these things to you? Maybe you told a friend, your mom, a sister?"

She motioned toward the diary. "It's all there, in writing. With dates. You said dates are good to have written down, right?"

He nodded and thumbed through the diary.

"The red ink," Rose said. "I wrote the entries that go along with the pictures in red ink."

As Raine watched Callum turn the pages, skimming entries, the amount of red ink had her stomach roiling with nausea.

Callum closed the diary and set it beside the envelopes. "One more question, Rose. In spite of Joey's abuse of you, you still testified to help him. The prosecutor even asked whether you felt Joey could have killed Alicia. You said no. Was that the truth?"

Her chin trembled, and the tears she'd been trying to hold back slid down her cheeks. "You have to understand. I loved Joey, but I was scared of him too. If I'd said anything bad on the stand, and he got out, came home…" She held her hands up in a helpless gesture. "I had to protect myself."

"Understood," Callum said. "But you have to say it. We need to hear it from you, in your own words. Do you think Joey Quintero had the opportunity, and could have killed Alicia Claremont?"

Rose picked up the smaller envelope and thumbed through the pictures. She paused, staring at one as she answered Callum.

"I went to bed before Joey came home the night Alicia was murdered. So I wasn't able to say whether he was with me at the time of her death. All I could say on the stand was that he was in bed when I woke up the next morning. I was honest about that, and everything else I testified about—except one thing. Do I think that Joey could have strangled and killed Alicia Claremont?" She set the picture down on the coffee table, faceup, the picture that showed the bruises around her throat. "Absolutely."

Chapter Nineteen

Callum stood beside the couch in his main room, his heart aching as Raine paced back and forth in front of him, venting about the case. At least she'd stopped crying. She'd cried most of the way to his house after Rose Garcia—the best character witness they had for her brother—declared in no uncertain terms that she believed he could have killed Alicia Claremont.

So far, Raine had refused to let him try to comfort her, not that he even knew how to do that. How could he make her feel better when everyone they'd spoken to either had nothing good to say about her brother, or something damning. She'd lost her parents and was about to lose her brother unless he figured out how to stop it.

But damned if he knew how at this point.

Raine stopped in front of him, her eyes red, dried tears forming tracks through her makeup. And she'd never looked more beautiful. He wanted to hold her, help her, somehow. But he'd learned in the past hour that she didn't want to be touched. Not now. Maybe not ever again if this week ended in the tragic way it appeared it was going to end.

"You heard what she said." Raine gestured help-lessly. "Rose defended Joey, said he would only hurt someone if he was drunk, or on drugs. But you and I have both read the police reports. No trace evidence. No DNA. And she was raped. A man out of his mind drunk doesn't put a condom on before he rapes someone. If Joey did it, he did it because he wanted to, not because he blacked out or was out of his mind with alcohol. He would have gotten drunk *after* he killed her. Not before."

"Raine—"

"Don't. Don't tell me it will all be okay. My God. Is he a killer? Is my brother a murderer after all? Have I been fooling myself this whole time?"

She started pacing back and forth again, so he didn't even try to answer what were likely rhetorical questions anyway. He didn't believe for a minute that she was ready to truly believe in Joey's guilt. She'd been supporting him and fighting for him for too long to cross that line right now. But she was struggling, because she was smart, and logical. Even a sister who desperately loved her brother couldn't deny the facts in front of her forever.

What they needed were more facts, something to turn the investigation completely around. The main problem he was encountering, of course, was that he wasn't convinced that her brother was innocent. Just the opposite. Even with Professor Kassin's doubts about the confession, every bit of circumstantial evidence pointed to Joey being the one who'd killed Alicia. And no evidence pointed to anyone else.

Or did it? Raine herself had said the police had zeroed in on Joey from the start—because he lived close by, had a rocky past and had allegedly been seen with Alicia in a bar.

By Randy Hagen.

"We've exhausted all avenues of trying to rehabilitate Joey as being innocent. The evidence just isn't there to sway anyone into changing their minds."

She stopped in front of him again, her gaze searching his. The look on her face was nothing short of devastation. "I never thought I'd hear you say that. I'm in the middle of a freak-out and you're giving up too?"

Unable to stop himself, he reached for her. When she didn't pull back this time, he cradled her against his chest and rested the top of his chin on her head.

"I'm not giving up. I'm accepting the facts we have right now, and switching gears. We need new facts. Instead of trying to prove that Joey could be innocent, we need to prove that someone else could have killed Alicia. We need to look at any viable suspects and try to create reasonable doubt. Right now, the only other person who seems a likely candidate to have killed her is Randy Hagen."

"Okay. Good, that's good. I've always said I didn't trust him, that he could have killed Alicia. But no one believed me."

"No one had any evidence to support that theory. We need to look for it. Sit down for a moment. Let's talk this through." He gently pushed her onto the couch facing him.

"Let's assume for a moment that he's the one who killed Alicia, that he lied when he testified, trying to frame Joey. You were investigating him on your own before you got my help. What did you do? Where did you go? Bars, right? That's why we theorized he might be the one who broke into your house, because he was mad that you and Joey's lawyers were asking questions about him in his hangout spots."

She nodded. "I visited every bar in town asking about him. It certainly wasn't a secret that I believed he'd lied on the stand about Joey."

"And then, when time was running out on Joey, you went to Gatlinburg looking for my help. Randy could have been forced to stay home to avoid questions by his friends in the bars. He didn't want this whole thing dragged up again. Maybe he drank himself into a rage and headed to your place, watched it off and on to see whether or not you were home. When he worked up enough courage, he broke in and tried to find your notes and files about him. When that didn't work out, because you'd taken everything with you to Gatlinburg, he trashed the place. He didn't expect us to pull up when he was still there, so he ran."

"You really think that's what happened?"

He shrugged. "It's a guess, an educated guess, but still just conjecture. It would make sense, though, if he was guilty, that he'd be worried about you digging up the case again. Now let's turn it around and assume he's not guilty."

"We're back to saying Joey killed Alicia?"

"No, not at all. We're brainstorming different angles to see what shakes loose. If we assume Hagen's not guilty, what's his motive for trashing your place, if he's the one who did it?" He already had an answer ready. But he wanted to shake her out of her feelings of helplessness. If he could get her reengaged with the case, she'd at least feel that she was contributing, and still cling to hope. Plus, she really was smart, a quick thinker. Maybe she *would* come up with something he hadn't thought of that could help.

"The perjury angle," she finally said. "Even if he's innocent of murder, if he lied on the stand about seeing Joey with Alicia at the bar, he committed perjury. If I had evidence of that, it could send him to prison. He'd be worried about me, innocent or guilty."

"Agreed," he said. "We need to look at him more in-depth. But we need to be careful. He could react like a cornered animal if he thinks we're onto him about the breaking and entering and he feels he has a lot to lose."

She shivered. "Okay. How do we, as you said, look into him? I got nothing from my inquiries."

"Let me guess. No one in the bars would talk to you?"

"Pretty much. Why would you assume that?"

He grinned. "Because you're a lawyer. No one in a bar wants to talk to a lawyer. They've all got their own sins to hide."

She rolled her eyes. "I'm a business lawyer. I don't handle criminal cases."

"The barflies don't understand the difference." He chuckled, then turned serious. "We need to look into Randy's alibi during the time that Alicia was killed. Do you remember his alibi? I don't remember reading about that in the police files. But I was focused more on Joey."

"So were the police. They barely looked at Randy after latching on to Joey as a suspect. Supposedly Randy was home. To his credit, Joey's trial defense attorney tried to explore Randy's alibi. But basically his story was that he was watching TV. His proof was that he gave the plot of the show he was watching. But everything is on demand these days, even back then. He could have watched it another time so he could speak to the plot."

"Excellent point. We can look into that. I wonder why the police accepted it so readily?"

"I guess because there wasn't any evidence pointing to him," she grudgingly admitted.

"Maybe. But given Farley's less-than-stellar reputation, there could be something more. Not that I think Farley would cover for someone he thought was guilty. I really don't see him doing that. But if he needed Randy's testimony to get who Farley thought was the bad guy, he may have done everything he could to ensure that Randy seemed like a credible witness. That includes propping up a weak alibi. We need to find out if there was another reason for them to put forth that alibi. Maybe they couldn't prove where Randy was at the time and came up with that story, again, so he could testify and be believable."

"That would be an awful thing to do."

"Hopefully that's not what happened. But we're exploring theoretical possibilities. Let me get Asher on it, have him run a criminal background report on Randy around the time of the murder. I'll have him run more than just local stuff, just to be extra thorough."

After giving Asher the assignment, Callum grabbed a quick snack of cheese and crackers for Raine and himself. Neither of them had felt like having lunch earlier. But now his stomach was starting to poke his ribs. Thankfully, he was able to coax her into eating some too. Emotions and stress would only get a person so far. He didn't want her getting sick and run-down because of this roller-coaster couple of weeks.

They'd just finished their snack when Asher called back. Callum was stacking their plates in the dishwasher and glanced across the kitchen island at Raine as he answered his phone.

"Hey, Asher. I've got you on speaker so Raine can hear. You have something for us already?"

"Thanks to our boss's amazing network of database access he's set up, I do. You're not going to believe this. Hagen's alibi is bogus. Completely made up. He wasn't home during the time of the murder."

Raine fist-pumped the air, but Callum shook his head in warning as he pushed for more information.

"Since the databases are law enforcement ones, and you're saying he wasn't home, I'm guessing he was in police custody at the time?"

Raine's eyes widened in dismay.

"Bingo," Asher said. "The Atlanta Police Department, over an hour away, had him locked up for public intoxication."

Raine slid onto a bar stool in front of the kitchen island. "He was in jail?"

"All night. He didn't kill Alicia, couldn't have."

She shook her head. "I don't understand. The police knew he was in jail, but they allowed him to use another alibi on the stand?"

"Not the Athens police," Asher said. "Atlanta police. It would depend on what type of search they did, how far they dug, as to whether they knew about his arrest."

"ACCPD knew," Callum said. "Randy wouldn't have risked being accused of murder. He'd have told them he had an airtight alibi. That means Farley, or the prosecutor, or both, covered for him. They knew that admitting he was in jail at the time made him a much less credible witness. They didn't want that coming out at trial. The jurors might not believe his testimony about seeing Joey with Alicia if they thought he wasn't credible."

Raine crossed her arms on top of the island. "So our hope that we might find another suspect we could argue had opportunity to kill Alicia is out. Hagen didn't kill her."

"No," Callum said. "He didn't. But we can prove he lied on the stand about his alibi. If he lied about one thing, he may have lied about another—like whether he saw your brother with Alicia. He's not the only bar patron who thought they might have seen them together, or at least Joey trying to talk to her. But he's the only one who swore at trial that it was definitely Joey. That's a piece of new, provable evidence—the first we've found. It's finally a start in the right direction. Thanks, Asher. Appreciate you jumping on that for us."

"You bet. If you need anything else, just call."

"I don't want to get too excited about this," Raine said. "It doesn't seem like enough to change the board's mind. Or am I not looking at it right?"

"I agree it probably wouldn't sway the board enough to grant a stay. But it might sway Randy. If we can find him, we may be able to convince him to admit he lied—assuming that he did—about Joey."

"Why would he agree to that?"

He smiled. "He wouldn't. Not on purpose, or at least not where someone in law enforcement would hear him. I'm thinking we try to interview him in a setting where he feels comfortable, and he's willing to brag about the truth, thinking we can't do anything about it. Maybe after a few beers."

"A bar. You want to interview him in a bar, and get him drunk."

"Loose, not drunk. What's that saying? Loose lips sink ships? We need to confirm whether his testimony about your brother is true or not. We've got nothing to lose, everything to gain."

She stood. "Okay, so we hit all the bars in town again. I know the ones that were his favorites back then. Those should be the first ones we try."

"You're not coming with me."

"What? Why not?"

"You already tried to find him earlier at the bars. Either he was there and snuck out the back when his friends saw you, or he heard you were looking for him and stayed away. I might have better luck on my own. He won't recognize me."

"He might if he's the one you chased in the woods behind my house."

He nodded. "There is that. But he was so busy try-ing to get away, I don't think he was trying to get a good look at my face. I'm the better choice for this particular task."

"Great. And what am I supposed to do while you go barhopping?"

He laughed. "I won't drink and have fun. Prom-ise." He stepped around to the other side of the island and gently grasped her shoulders. "You've had a re-ally rough day, Raine. Take this as a welcome break. Maybe try to have a nap, or eat something more than crackers. You haven't been eating well at all."

"Careful, Callum. You're sounding awfully con-cerned about a lawyer."

His smile broadened. "I'm currently rethinking my animosity toward lawyers, or at least one in par-ticular." When she didn't smile, he sighed heavily. "My charm isn't working today."

"What charm?" She arched a brow.

"Ouch. I'll have to work on that. In the meantime, like I said, take a break. And keep trusting me. You chose the right man for the job. Let me do what I do.

And let me do it without distractions, without worrying about your safety."

He gave her a quick kiss, then hurried toward the carport entry before he did something stupid, like *really* kiss her. Now wasn't the time. She was vulnerable, not necessarily thinking clearly after the stress of today. And they'd agreed to keep it professional between them, to focus on the case. But dang it was hard. What he really wanted to do, more than anything right now, was hold her and somehow chase away all the hurts and fears. But he wasn't strong enough to do that without wanting more. Much more.

A few minutes down the road, his phone pinged. He expected to see Asher's number on the screen again, perhaps giving him another update. Instead, he was surprised to see his friend Noah Reid's number.

"Hey, Noah. It's great to hear from you again. But I'm kind of busy right now, working the Quintero case. Can we catch up later?"

"Absolutely. I want to try the fishing out there in your pond again. But that's not why I called."

As Callum listened, he stiffened in surprise. "You're kidding. Okay, yes." He checked the time on his watch. "I can make it. Might be a couple of minutes late, but I'll be there."

Callum hung up and immediately called Asher. "Hey, man. I need your help. Can you get some local PIs on the search for Hagen? He's more at home in a bar than his place. Shouldn't be too hard to find him if someone he's not familiar with subtly puts out feelers. I don't think he's high on ACCPD's priority list or they'd have located him by now. I was going to look for him, but something else has come up."

"Sure, okay. I know a few guys I can call. Maybe a gal too, someone pretty who might have better luck getting his attention. What do you want done once they locate him?"

Callum quickly explained his goal of getting Randy to admit he lied—if he lied. "And make sure when he leaves that someone tails him. I don't want him going anywhere near my place in Athens while Raine's there alone."

"You're not with her? Where are you?"

"On my way to Jackson Prison."

Chapter Twenty

Raine finished straightening up the kitchen, not that there was a lot to clean. Callum kept everything neat and orderly, a man after her own heart. But she washed down the countertops, making sure to get any crumbs.

The sound of the carport door to the house opening surprised her. Callum had only been gone a few minutes. He must have forgotten something. The door clicked closed behind her as she tossed a paper towel into the garbage.

"I thought he'd never leave."

She whirled around at the sound of the unfamiliar voice. A man stood about ten feet away, dressed all in black. He was tall and muscular, like Callum. But unlike Callum, he was blond and pale, as if he spent most of his time indoors.

Dark eyes stared back at her with a disturbing, feral intensity. Then he smiled, a cold, cruel smile. And she started to shake.

"Who are you? What do you want?"

"Ah, that's right. You haven't met me yet, have

you, dear? Maybe you haven't even heard about me. You and that investigator you hired have been focused on the Scoggin fellow." His lip curled in a sneer. "Trying to give him credit for one of my kills. You got him in a tizzy by performing surveillance on him. He wrote down your license plate number, figured out who you were. When more investigators showed up, watching him, he knew you must have been behind it."

She grasped the edge of the kitchen island, her whole body shaking now. "Credit for your kills? You mean Nancy? You killed her?"

"I killed them all, darlin'. Including Nancy. And I didn't appreciate hearing on the news that Scoggin was wanted for her death. I work hard on my projects. I may not want anyone knowing they were mine. You know, the whole prison thing. But someone else taking credit, well, I can't have that. But I'm getting ahead of myself. Raine Quintero, I'm Drake Knox. And the pleasure, I assure you, is about to be all mine."

His smile widened, showing perfect white teeth that reminded her more of a badger's than a human being's. "And I must say, I'm flattered by how white your face just turned. You must have heard of me after all."

Her gun. She had to get her gun. It was in the guest bedroom, in the side table drawer. Could she reach it before he reached her?

She inched her way around the island, toward the family room. He arched a brow as he watched, not the least bit concerned, which made her even more terrified. Images of his victims, the police photos she'd bribed a clerk to give her, appeared in her mind's eye. All had been strangled to death. But before that, their killer had tortured them. The coroners in each case had theorized the victims had been bound, cut, beaten and raped. For hours.

She had to get her gun. Distraction. She needed a distraction.

"Are you saying Scoggin trashed my house?"

He cocked his head like a bird watching a worm wriggling on the ground, just before he snatched it up. And killed it.

"Let me guess," he said. "You thought it was that silly Hagen fellow. Low-life little criminal whose entire résumé consists of petty theft and drunk driving. That sort of thing. I can see him trashing your place, I suppose. But once your shenanigans got Scoggin in the limelight, well, he just couldn't control his temper."

She reached the end of the island. She was about fifteen feet away from him now. He still hadn't moved.

"How…how do you know all of this?" One step away from the island, toward the family room part of the open concept room. Could she get the couch in between them before she took off running for the bedroom?

He smiled, seemingly amused as she dared to take another step toward the couch. "My apologies for the confusion, Raine. Can I call you Raine?" He waved a hand, as if waving away his question. "Of course I'll call you Raine. After all, we're about to become great...friends."

Oh, God. Please help me. Another step. Why wasn't he moving? Why did he seem so confident that she wasn't going to get away? It didn't matter. She had to get that gun. Another step.

His only reaction to her movements was to continue watching her, and to put his hands in the pockets of his black jacket. "I should clarify, instead of starting in the middle of the story. Scoggin went on the run, that whole BOLO thing—after trashing your place. As luck would have it, the minute I heard on the news that he was wanted for my work, I looked into his past and figured out he had a cabin up in the mountains. Or, to be more accurate, his ex-wife did. She got it in the divorce. I figured he'd head there if he wanted to hide, rather than to his own home or places he was known to frequent. So I went there first, and waited. Let's just say he was quite forthcoming in answering all of my questions."

She took another step, and swallowed, hard. "You killed him?"

"Of course."

Her stomach dropped at how casually he spoke about murdering someone. "And Hagen too I'm guessing."

He rolled his eyes. "Hagen isn't worth a thought in my head. Scoggin, on the other hand, as I already explained, had to be taken care of."

"What does this have to do with me? I've never done anything to you."

He frowned, looking aggravated. "You're not listening. Scoggin. You're the reason I was forced to stray from my plans for UB to take care of Scoggin."

She blinked. "Your plans for UB? I don't understand."

He watched her take another step. Twenty feet away now. She'd reached the opposite end of the couch. Did she dare try to gain the last few feet to the entrance of the hallway before she took off running?

"I've been keeping an eye on the Unfinished Business team for months, ever since the local police announced that UB was going to take on my cold cases, investigate my kills. And I've been tracking them the same way I track my victims. I have GPS locators on some of their vehicles. Including your boyfriend, Mr. Wright's. Have for a while now, even before he came to Athens."

He laughed. "Isn't that funny? You finally find your Mr. Right, pun intended, and you'll never be able to have that bright shiny future you've probably fantasized about since you were a little girl. It's how I knew he was staying here. I've been watching you, and was delighted that you were both together. First, I'll take care of you, for causing me such trouble. Then, when your prince charming arrives, I'll take care of him."

She took off running.

A crackling, sizzling sound filled the air. Something hit her between the shoulder blades. Blinding hot pain shot through every nerve in her body, dropping her gasping and writhing to the floor.

Chapter Twenty-One

It was well past dark by the time Callum started up the long driveway to his Athens home. He was worried about Raine. He'd tried calling her several times on his way here but she hadn't answered. Likely it was nothing. She could be taking that nap he'd recommended, or a long, hot bath. Or maybe she was out fiddling with the plants in the backyard as she often liked to do to de-stress, and had left her phone inside. She'd done it before, which was the only reason he hadn't called his brother-in-law to drive the half hour from town to check on her.

But now that he was almost there, an itchy feeling started in his shoulder blades. She'd never not answered his calls this long before.

Short of the last turn, he parked beneath some trees and killed the lights. When he got out of the SUV, he quietly pushed the door closed rather than let it slam shut. Crouching down, he made his way to the last group of trees before the clearing around the house.

As usual, the lights shone from the backyard. And

landscape lighting lit up the beddings and ornamental trees in the front. But the house itself was dark.

Forgoing another call, he sent her a text this time.

Sweetheart, I'm on the way home. Should be there in about an hour. Will you wait up for me?

A minute later, a reply popped onto his screen.

I'm up. See you soon.

He swore and punched the speed dial for his brother-in-law. "Danny, hey, it's Callum. Something's wrong at my house. I think Raine may be in trouble."

"You think? What's going on?"

He explained about the text. "I've never called her sweetheart. And she didn't say a thing about it. Someone else must have her phone."

"That's weak, Callum. You're a half hour out of town and—"

"Asking my brother-in-law and former partner to trust me on this. Something's wrong. Send help. No lights. No sirens. Use the element of surprise. You know someone recently broke into her home. I think they're here right now, with her."

"Hagen?"

"No. The guy we sent looking for him found him and is tailing him. It's not Hagen. Could be Scoggin." Or worse. He prayed it wasn't worse. "Just get someone out here. Hurry. And bring an ambulance too. Just in case."

"Okay, okay. I'm on it. Wait for backup. Keep an eye on the place and call me if the situation changes before we get there."

Callum hung up without answering. Waiting for backup wasn't an option. He silenced the phone, then drew his gun. He'd keep an eye on the situation, from the inside. No way in hell was he waiting out here if Raine was in trouble.

RAINE'S RESPECT FOR police officers who voluntarily got tased as part of their training had gone up a thousand percent. Being tased hurt beyond anything she'd ever experienced. And it wasn't the five-second ride she heard cops talk about. Knox had pressed the trigger over and over until she'd screamed and begged for mercy, or tried to through clenched teeth.

His version of mercy was to rip the Taser darts out of her back and handcuff her to a bar stool in the middle of the living room. Naked. And bleeding. Because the sicko had a love for knives as well.

Funny how after the first few cuts, the others didn't hurt as much. And too bad Callum's bar stools weren't the kind with arms and backs. She could have tried that neat trick of his, holding up the arms of the bar stool and smashing it on the floor to break free. Except that her ankles were cuffed to the legs of the stool too. That wouldn't work. Why was she so warm? Naked and warm was weird, wasn't it? Unless you were in a shower. Shouldn't she be cold? Maybe it was the blood, smeared on her skin, warming her.

Hot shooting pain snapped her head back. She whimpered and forced her eyes open.

"Welcome back." Knox grinned and lowered his hand. "Had to slap you pretty hard that time. Stop going to la-la land. We've barely started our fun."

"What did your mother ever do to you to make you such a sicko?"

He growled like a feral animal and slapped her again. She cried out in pain and the world suddenly tilted.

Knox swore and grabbed her, setting the stool back on all four legs and straightening her on it. "This may not be my best idea," he admitted, sounding disgusted. "What idiot uses bar stools and doesn't have a table and chairs?"

"This idiot."

Knox whirled around, but he wasn't fast enough. Callum slammed into him, knocking him to the floor.

Raine cried out as the stool tilted again. It fell over against the couch, knocking her head on the arm, hard. The scuffling and grunting on the floor close by told her Knox and Callum were in an all-out brawl—one fighting to save her, one fighting to kill her.

She blinked through the dark fog trying to pull her under. *Stay conscious. You have to help Callum.* She dragged in a ragged breath and slapped her cheeks, hoping the pain would clear her head. Slapped her cheeks? She stared in wonder at her hands, the handcuffs dangling from both wrists. They weren't cuffed to the bar stool anymore. When she pushed against the couch, she realized why. The stool had broken during her fall.

Her ankles were still cuffed to what remained of the legs of the stool, but she could move around.

Gun. Hadn't she been getting her gun when Knox stunned her? If she could get it, she could help Callum and—

"Raine, look out!"

She jerked around just as a knife came slashing down at her. It missed her by mere inches and the momentum sent Knox crashing to the floor again.

"Move, move," Callum yelled, as he lunged toward Knox.

She grasped the back of the couch and used all her strength to pull herself over it, dragging the broken stool with her. When she hit the floor on the other side, the rest of the stool shattered like kindling, bits of it scraping against her. It didn't even hurt. And she wasn't warm anymore. She was cold, her teeth chattering together.

"Well, shoot," she mumbled, her tongue feeling oddly thick. "Wait. *Shoot.* I need my gun." She pushed herself up on her hands and knees, pieces of wood clinging like a spider to her left calf. She swore and kicked at it, then fell again. Her arms and legs weren't working right.

So cold.

A deafening scream sounded from the other side of the couch. Then everything went quiet.

Raine lay there, not sure what to do.

Her teeth chattered again. "C-C-Callum?"

He was suddenly there beside her, looking down at her with such fear in his eyes that she wondered if Knox was behind her. She tried to look over her shoulder.

"Where is he?"

"Dead. Oh, honey. What did he do to you?" His hands shook as he searched for injuries.

Suddenly the front door and carport door burst open at the same time. "Police, don't move!"

She strained to see Callum in the chaos as people raced inside. One minute he was there, the next he wasn't. "Callum? Where did you go?"

She heard swearing and cursing, a scuffle.

"Let him go. He's my brother-in-law, the guy who called me for help."

Was that Detective Cooper's voice? Danny?

Callum's face appeared over hers again. A blanket seemed to magically be in his hands and he covered her with it, pressing down on her belly.

"Don't, that hurts," she cried out, pushing at his hands.

"I'm so sorry, sweetheart. I have to stop the bleeding. You've got a really bad cut on your belly."

"Don't call me sweetheart."

"There's my girl. Okay, honey. I won't call you sweetheart."

She laughed, then clutched his hands over her middle. "Ouch."

"Get that ambulance here, now!" Callum yelled.

"Two minutes out," Danny told him.

"You'll be okay, Raine. Just hold on. Hold on."

She clutched his jacket. "I'm holding on. You hold on too. Don't let me go." She coughed, then gasped, her face white with pain.

"Easy, Raine. I've got you. I won't let go."

She smiled, then closed her eyes and went limp.

Chapter Twenty-Two

The doorbell chime had Raine glancing up from her computer. Callum was early. They weren't due to leave for another forty-five minutes. Maybe he wanted to arrive even earlier than they'd planned. Could he be as nervous as she was about speaking to the prison board?

No. She smiled at that ridiculous thought. Callum wouldn't be nervous. He was always confident and capable, even when facing certain death. He'd saved her from Knox a few days ago. And she had faith that if anyone could save her brother today, it was Callum. This was Joey's last chance. His only chance. If this didn't work, he'd be executed this evening.

Tears started in her eyes. She brushed them away and drew a shaky breath. *Good thoughts. Think good thoughts. We're going to save him. We have to.*

As she pushed up from her chair in her home office, she sucked in a sharp breath. Her injuries made her stiff and sore. But she was grateful and thankful to be alive. The wounds would heal. Again, thanks to Callum.

She shuffled down the hallway beneath the stairs toward the foyer. Just before she reached the door, the doorbell chimed again.

"Just a second," she called out, flipping the top dead bolt, then a second one, thanks to his thoughtfulness. She still couldn't believe that he'd hired someone to clean her house, replace all of the destroyed items and reinforce every door and window with new locks right after her home had been broken into. He'd had all of that done while the two of them were running all over the place interviewing witnesses, and she hadn't even known about it.

"Did you check the peephole before unlocking the door?" Callum called out.

She smiled and looked through the peephole, even though she didn't need to. Then she opened the door. Callum in a business suit was devastating, even more so than Callum in jeans. How had she not been this affected seeing him in a suit before? He was gorgeous, in anything.

She let out a shaky breath, and tried hard not to stare. Now wasn't the time. Maybe later, hopefully, they could talk, see where this…thing between them was going. But first, Joey. They had to be successful today. She couldn't even consider the alternative.

"You're early," she said. "The appointment isn't until two o'clock."

His smile didn't quite reach his eyes. "I wanted to check on you. It's only been a couple of days since… since what happened. Are you feeling okay? You really should have stayed in the hospital more than one day."

"I'm fine. I fainted from blood loss. You keep acting like I almost died."

"You *did* almost die."

"No. I was almost murdered, but you prevented Knox from doing that. Big difference. Stop worrying about me. Is that why you came early? To mother hen me?"

He smiled again, barely. "That, and to make sure that everything was fixed the way you wanted it."

"My house? Are you kidding? It's better than new. I still can't believe you won't let me reimburse you. But I sincerely appreciate what you did. After Knox…well, it was wonderful being able to come home from the hospital and not have to worry about the repairs. Thank you."

"Of course. What about you, though? Are you sure you're okay? Feeling good enough to make the trip to Jackson Prison? After everything you've been through—"

She put her hand on his arm. "Nothing will keep me from being there today. Stop worrying about me. I'm alive and perfectly fine. Bruised, with a few minor cuts here and there, but—"

"Minor?" He swore. "You had thirty-seven stitches. That's not minor."

"I can't believe you kept track of the total. But the worst cut only needed twelve."

He blanched. "Good grief. If I hadn't already killed the bastard I'd kill him again."

"He'd have done far worse than some punches and cuts if you hadn't saved me. That's exactly what you did, you know. You saved me, and the lives of other women he'd have gone on to torture and murder if you and your team hadn't figured out he was the serial killer. It's over. Let it go. I have."

His jaw tightened, but he gave her a curt nod. "I wanted to update you about Hagen too."

She motioned toward the family room. "We don't have to stand. There's still plenty of time before we have to leave. Come sit on the couch with me."

He hesitated, as if he was going to tell her no. But then he nodded again and followed her across the room. She made a concerted effort to move as normally as possible so he wouldn't start fussing about her injuries again. Getting up and sitting were the hardest parts. But she forced a smile through the pain as she lowered herself to the couch.

When he chose a wing chair instead of sitting beside her, she couldn't help the twinge of disappointment. But it was the new worry lines on his forehead that had her attention.

"Callum, if you're still concerned about me, don't be. I'm really okay. Promise."

"I'll always be concerned about you, Raine. But there are a few more updates that I need to give you." He ran a hand through his short hair, a gesture she'd never seen him do before.

"What's going on, Callum? You're making me nervous, even more than I already was with today being Joey's board review." She refused to mention the elephant in the room, that it was also the day that Joey was scheduled to die.

He winced. "That's what I wanted to update you about. The board review. Even though the investigator Asher hired got Hagen to swear out an affidavit that he'd lied about seeing Joey with Alicia, the prosecutor is refusing to pursue perjury charges against him. His reasoning is that other witnesses said they thought they saw Joey with Alicia too. Even though they didn't swear they were positive about that under oath, the sheer number of witnesses who gave statements that they thought they saw him is overwhelming, again in the prosecutor's opinion. He doesn't feel it would have made a difference in Joey's ultimate conviction, even if Hagen hadn't lied."

Her stomach knotted. "If the prosecutor doesn't think Hagen's retraction would make a difference, what are our chances that the board will?"

He cleared his throat. "About that. I'm not going to try to talk you out of meeting with the board—"

"I should hope not. Wait, talk *me* out of meeting with them? We're *both* going before them." She searched his eyes, her stomach twisting even more. "Aren't we?"

"In good conscience, no. I can't speak to them on your brother's behalf."

She stared at him in shock. "I don't... I don't understand. Why not?"

His tortured gaze met hers. "Because I believe that your brother killed Alicia Claremont."

Before she could catch her breath over that statement, he continued.

"I agree with the prosecutor. Hagen's retraction isn't strong enough to convince me that a jury wouldn't have convicted him, even without Hagen's testimony. No other viable suspects are on anyone's radar. Joey's the only one who could have killed her. He had motive, and opportunity."

"What about an as-yet-unknown stranger as the perpetrator? Strangers do home invasions and kill people they don't know. Look at Knox, for goodness' sake. He didn't know any of the women he murdered. It does happen. The police just haven't found the right suspect yet."

"There's no forensic evidence that a stranger was involved—"

"And there's no forensic evidence that Joey was involved," she countered, hating the desperation in her voice.

He sighed. "Alicia wouldn't have opened her door to someone she didn't know that late at night. And there was no sign of a break-in. She'd met Joey in the bar—"

"No. She didn't." She clutched her hands together again. "Hagen retracted."

"Other people saw them, as we've discussed. And you saw Rose's diary, those pictures. You saw what he did to her. You heard her say that even though she deeply loved Joey, she was convinced he could kill. We spoke to other witnesses from the trial, including experts, and no one has changed their opinions or their stories since their very first statements years ago. Your biggest argument for him is that his confession was coerced. The leading expert on false confessions said she couldn't conclude that it had been."

"She couldn't conclude that it hadn't been either."

"Raine—"

"Stop. Stop trying to convince me that my brother is a killer." She wrapped her arms around her middle.

"I don't mean to try to convince you of that. It was never my intention to take your belief in his innocence away from you."

"Then what *is* your intention?"

"I want you to understand my beliefs, that I have a different view of what happened than you do. And I want you to understand why I can't go against those beliefs. More than anything, I'd hoped I could find proof of his innocence. I wanted to give you that gift, to make you happy. But I can't."

"I gambled everything, I gambled my brother's life, on you helping me save him. And now you're refusing to do the one thing I absolutely needed you to do—talk to the prison board and tell them he's innocent."

"From the very beginning, our agreement was that I would investigate, that I would search for the truth. And if I didn't find anything to point to his innocence, I was done. I never lied about that."

She squeezed her hands together so hard they ached. "If you do this, Callum, if you refuse to go with me and speak to them about the outstanding questions, the doubts, Hagen's retraction, then it's just me. His sister. Pleading for his life. What kind of chance would I have? A family member doesn't have the credibility that you would. I need you. I need your expertise, your reputation in law enforcement. Callum, I'm begging you. Please. Just talk to them."

"I already have."

Her world tilted on its axis as terror flooded through her veins. "What are you saying?"

"I met with them early this morning and gave my full report."

"I don't... Full report? Why didn't you wait and go with me? What report are you talking about? You're not making sense. My God, Callum. What did you tell them?"

His pain-filled gaze searched hers. "The truth. I told them the truth, that I investigated his case and found nothing to justify me arguing on his behalf. I'm still taking you to your appointment. I don't want you going through all of this alone at the prison, especially if, well. I'll drive you there, go with you inside, be there for you afterward. But I won't go before the board and try to convince them of his innocence. I'm sorry. I can't."

"Get out," she rasped, her voice breaking. "Get out of my house. I never want to see you again. Ever."

"Raine, don't do this. We—"

"Get out!"

He stared at her a long moment, then stood. "I'm sorry. I truly am. If you need anything—"

"What I need, you refuse to give. Go."

He sighed, then headed toward the door. "Good-bye, Raine."

She ignored him, refusing to look his way.

The door opened, then shut with a firm click.

She crumpled into a ball and gave in to the sobs she'd been fighting to hold back.

Chapter Twenty-Three

Raine stood at her back doors, looking out at the view of the preservation area that once had given her peace. Now nothing gave her peace.

Three months ago, her world had been filled with new hope and possibilities. But a lot had happened in those three months.

Callum had betrayed her.

The board denied her appeal.

Her brother was murdered by the state.

She drew a ragged breath, the pain still so fresh it was as if it had all happened yesterday. Not the physical pain, the wounds that Knox had inflicted. Those were mostly healed. It was the anguish, the heartache that she doubted would ever heal.

So much had been left unsaid. Her brother had refused to even talk to her the day of his execution. Instead, he'd sent a brief note saying he loved her and to please remember him kindly. That was it. How was she supposed to heal the hole in her heart with a stupid note?

And how was she supposed to move forward when there was another hole to fill, the one left by Callum?

She blew out a long breath, then turned to study the progress she'd made in the past week. Most everything was packed into boxes and labeled either to be given to charity or to go into storage. The few things she was keeping would go with her. There was nothing left for her here. Her parents were gone. Her brother was gone. The long hours she'd dedicated to work and to the fight to save Joey had deprived her of any close friends. And the fulfillment she used to get from her job had evaporated. She'd resigned, cutting the last link she had with Athens.

Well, except for the Claremonts.

They'd always been so kind to her. Even when she'd told them that she'd finally accepted her brother's guilt, and apologized for the pain her ignorance and Joey's horrible actions had caused them, they only offered love and support in return. Never any judgment or condemnation. But even though they'd no doubt welcome her if she went to see them in the future, she didn't plan to ever darken their doorstep again. It was time to let the past go. It was time to move on, literally.

If she was going to live again, to find joy again, somehow she had to find a new purpose in her life. Saving Joey had been the impetus behind almost every adult decision she'd made. Without that need, that drive, she was floundering. Lost. And ashamed.

Because she missed Callum far more than she did her brother.

She'd loved Joey, still did. But time had a way

of clearing the veils she'd had over her eyes for so long. Had they ever really been close? No. He was dating and partying when she was still in elementary school. They hadn't seen each other much growing up because he moved out on his own while she was still living with their parents. But he was all she had. And when that was threatened, she'd dedicated her life to fixing the wrong, to getting justice. But she was no longer sure what justice meant in Joey's case.

Everything Callum and the other investigators at Unfinished Business had found only supported her brother's guilt and reinforced what was said in the trial. And her brother had confessed. Was she too blinded by her own determination to see the truth? Her heart said no. But her mind, her logic, that supposed intelligence Callum had admired, all said something completely different.

That Joey had murdered Alicia Claremont.

She scanned the boxes piled high in her family room again. What was she going to do next? Where was she going to go? How would she ever find peace and happiness in the wreckage that her life had become?

The doorbell chimed, startling her. She certainly wasn't expecting anyone. It was probably a salesman who'd managed to sneak past the guard at the gate. It wouldn't be the first time.

She headed to the front door and looked through the peephole. A trim dark-skinned man in a light gray business suit stood there, a black leather satchel in his hand.

"Yes?" she called out.

"Ma'am, Ms. Quintero, my name is Noah Reid. Callum Wright may have mentioned me?"

She blinked, then slowly opened the door. "Mr. Reid. You're the one who helped Callum and me get to see my brother without having to wade through red tape. Thank you."

He smiled. "It's always my pleasure to help Callum. I'm forever in his debt. He saved my life once, nearly died himself doing it. Did he tell you about that?"

She shook her head. "No. He didn't."

"Well, that's a story for another day." His smile faded. "My condolences about your brother. I'm so sorry for your loss."

"I appreciate that."

He held up the satchel. "If you have a few minutes, there are some things that I feel you should know."

"Oh, of course. Where are my manners? Come in, please."

RAINE STOOD ON the unfamiliar porch checking the address on her phone one more time. This was the right place. But no one had answered her repeated knocks and ringing of the doorbell. She was sure she'd heard voices at some point. Maybe they were in the backyard? She'd come too far not to at least check.

She followed the stone pathway that led around the side of the garage toward the back of the property. There wasn't a fence, which was common in Gatlinburg. No one wanted to block their gorgeous views of the mountains. And as she rounded the garage, she could certainly appreciate the one here. The snow-covered mountaintops towered in the distance, and yet they felt close enough to touch. Beautiful.

"Raine?"

She turned with a smile to face Callum.

And the blonde woman beside him, holding his hand.

Her smile faltered. "I, ah, I'm sorry. I was trying to surprise you, but, ah, you've got company. I'll go." She turned and hurried down the side of the garage, humiliation scorching her cheeks. He'd moved on, and she was an idiot.

"Raine, wait." Strong hands grabbed her shoulders, then gently turned her around. Callum stared down at her, his gaze searching hers as he cupped her face. "Is it really you, or am I dreaming?"

"More like a nightmare." She pushed his hands away. "My fault. I shouldn't have shown up like this. I'll leave you to your…whatever she is." She turned around again.

"You mean my sister? Lucy?"

She stopped, then slowly turned to face him. "That woman? She's—"

"Lucy Cooper, Danny's wife. My sister. She and Danny came for a visit."

"And we were just leaving," a feminine voice said behind him. Lucy stepped around Callum and smiled. "My husband's pulling up right now out front. He just filled the tank for our trip back to Athens." She held out her hand. "You must be Raine. Callum has told me a lot about you."

"Lucy, don't," he warned.

"Don't what, brother? Tell her you can't stop talking about her?"

Raine glanced at him in surprise as she shook Lucy's hand. "You've been talking about me?"

"All good things," Lucy assured her. "Nice meeting you. Hope to see you again." She stood on tiptoe and kissed Callum's cheek. "Don't be a stranger. I mean it. We expect a visit this summer, if not before."

"We'll see." He was talking to his sister, but watching Raine the whole time.

Lucy chuckled. "Well, I can tell I'll be missed." She was still laughing as she moved past them and disappeared around the corner.

A moment later, the fading sound of a car engine indicated she and Danny had left and were heading down the mountain.

"How did you find where I live?" Callum asked.

"Asher."

"He never could keep a secret."

She shifted on her feet and tugged her jacket closer. "Could we go inside, where it's warm? It's much colder here in the mountains than in Athens."

"Oh, of course. Sorry. I'm just...surprised to see you." He led the way around the back and opened the sliding glass door for her to enter.

She stepped inside, barely registering the interior other than to take the nearest seat—which happened to be his couch. As he sat beside her, she turned to face him.

"It's nice to see that you're back in touch with your sister. How did that happen?"

"She contacted me a month ago to let me know my father was dying."

"Oh no. I'm so sorry."

"If I hadn't had you as an example of how to be supportive of family, no matter what, I'd have hung up on her. Instead, I bit the bullet and went and saw him. It's because of you that I was able to look past my stubborn pride and reconnect with him, with my family. We made our peace before Dad passed away. And I'm trying to rebuild the bridges with my relatives. Again, thanks to you." He stared intently at her. "Are you okay? I heard…about your brother, that your appeal with the board was unsuccessful. I really am sorry."

She swallowed and forced a smile.

"Is that why you're here? Your brother?"

"What do you… Oh, you mean to berate you or something? Blame you for him being executed?"

He winced. "It would be your right."

"No, Callum. It wouldn't be my right. You did everything you could to try to find something to show he was innocent. You did that for me, and I appreciate it, in spite of how poorly I behaved the last time I saw you."

His brow wrinkled in confusion. "Raine, I'm a bit lost. Why, exactly, are you here if not to curse me for betraying you?"

She sighed and reached into her purse, then pulled out a sheaf of papers. "I'm here about these."

He took them and scanned the first page, then the

next, then shuffled through the rest before tossing them onto the coffee table. "How did you get those?"

"Your friend. Noah Reid."

He swore. "You were never supposed to see them."

"Why? Why would you not want me to see the documentation that absolutely one hundred percent proves my brother did kill Alicia Claremont?"

His jaw tightened but he didn't say anything.

"That day that Knox came after me, you went to the prison. Reid said he'd called you with information he'd been working to gather on my brother's case. And you went to look into that information and even spoke to my brother. No less than a dozen former cellmates of his, along with some prison guards, gave affidavits saying Joey confessed several times to them over the years that he killed Alicia. The kicker is that you spoke to Joey that day, and he…" A sob caught in her throat.

Callum's gaze filled with anguish. "Don't. Don't do this to yourself. I never wanted you to experience this pain."

"Joey confessed to you that day. He bragged about the kill, described the flowers on the back of Mrs. Claremont's closet, those books we found in Alicia's drawer, those glow-in-the-dark stars on her bedroom ceiling, other things not in police reports or in crime scene photos. The guard overheard him. That's what one of those papers says. My brother couldn't have known those details unless he was the killer. That's why you told the prison board you weren't convinced of his innocence. That's why you wouldn't stand with me before them to plead for his life. What I don't un-derstand is why you didn't show me the affidavits. Why not tell me the truth? If I'd known he was truly guilty, beyond a doubt, I wouldn't have gone to the board to argue for a stay."

He took her hands in his, his thumbs rubbing slow, gentle circles across the backs. "Because you were in denial. It was too much to deal with at the time. And I didn't want to destroy your last moments with your brother. I wanted you to have good memories of him. But I couldn't lie to the board either, and be the one responsible for him perhaps one day going back into society. It was a fine line to walk. I did what my conscience dictated. But I wanted to protect you too. Or, at least, I tried."

"Don't you see, Callum? You did protect me. Over and over again. From Knox, from things too painful for me to bear at the time. But I know the truth now, and I'm at peace with it. And I thank God that you followed your conscience. Because the real tragedy would have been if I'd managed to get Joey eventu-ally released and he killed again. That's something I don't think I could have lived with. So, you see, once again you saved me. I was just too blind to see it at the time. But I see it now. And I'm here to beg for your forgiveness."

He stared at her in wonder. "You don't hate me?"

Tears dripped down her cheeks as she tightened her hands on his. "Maybe I did, or thought I did, at first. But even before Reid came to my house to give me those papers, I'd let go of the hate, the anger. And I was desperately lonely for you. I was on my way back to you without even realizing it. All Reid did was give me an excuse. I love you, Callum Wright. I love you with all my heart. I just hope I haven't destroyed any chance that you might one day grow to love me too."

A beautiful smile bloomed on his face, lightening his expression and filling his eyes with happiness. And hope. And something else she was too afraid to name in case she was wrong.

"I love you too, Raine Quintero. I think I've loved you since the moment I found out you pointed an unloaded gun at me." He grinned.

"I wasn't wrong about what I saw in your eyes," she whispered through her tears.

"What?"

"Just kiss me, sweetheart. Kiss me and never let me go."

He laughed. "Okay, honey. For better or worse."

Her eyes widened as she stared up at him. "Better or worse?"

He winked. "Until death do us part. If you'll have me."

"If that's a proposal, it's the worst one ever."

"Marry me anyway?"

"Yes, yes, yes." She threw her arms around him and he kissed her.

And never let her go.

* * * * *

Look for more books in
A Tennessee Cold Case Story miniseries
by Lena Diaz, coming soon!

And if you missed the previous titles
in the series, look for:

Murder on Prescott Mountain
Serial Slayer Cold Case
Shrouded in the Smokies

Available now from Harlequin Intrigue!

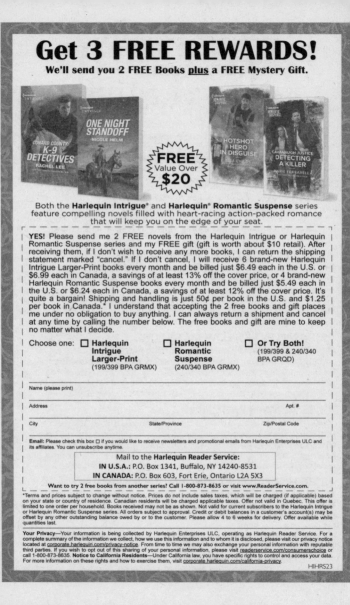

HARLEQUIN
PLUS

Try the best multimedia
subscription service for romance
readers like you!

Read, Watch and Play.

Experience the easiest way to get
the romance content you crave.

Start your **FREE TRIAL** at
<u>www.harlequinplus.com/freetrial</u>.